SACRIFICED

Jeni Burns

Sacrificed

Twisted Fate Novella #2

Cover Design By: Valentine Pinova

ISBN:1-942964-03-X

ISBN-13:978-1-942964-03-2

ACKNOWLEDGEMENTS

There are so many people to thank for their support and guidance along this journey, but some that must be mentioned are as follows:

First, a special thanks to Ron, E and A for being the magic in my days and the stars in my nights.

Thank you to my in-laws for helping Ron with the kids so I can work. I'm eternally grateful to you both.

Thank you to all of my amazing writing and critique partners (N.R., D.L., R.P., J.S, S.H., E.R., A.M., D.M.W., & T.P.).

To Reagan Phillips, Denise Leton, and N.R. Ratcliffe, I swear I couldn't do this without the three of you. From the drunk octopus issues to the squirrel themed texts, you all hold a very special place in my heart.

Also, a huge 'thank you' to all the members of Carolina Romance Writers. This wonderful group of writers is uplifting, supportive, and comforting. There will never be a writing group as fun and exciting as you guys.

A huge 'thank you' to Lara Stokes who has had the patience to listen to every potential plot point and not be upset when I change it at the last minute. An equally grand 'thank you' to Lauriel Faltin for jotting me notes via text while juggling so many other things.

One last note of thanks goes out to Dayanara Lorenzo, Jamie Pejo, Brenda Onley, & Gail Onley for always being the family I needed but wasn't born into.

Thank you to Valentine Pinova for the amazing cover art.

Thanks to all the amazing people at Rush Espresso who put up with my decaf habit and are always quick to smile even before I've had my first sip. You guys rock.

A huge 'thank you' to everyone who helped edit including, Jan Carol, Help Me Edit Editing Services, and Joshua Strecker. Without these amazingly talented professionals, I'd be in a padded room, still wondering where the commas go. Thank you all for being amazing.

With all my thanks,

~ j

To Steven Taylor with love.

For daring to dream big on my behalf and
believing I could fly.

You give me wings.

ONE

EARLY 1900's

DRAMMELECH DEWSBERRY HAD wandered through every inch of New Jersey for over two hundred years; angry, bitter, tired. Over the years, he'd left a trail of bodies in his wake; pretty young things, all with their veins turned black. That was until he happened upon a witch—a witch who would get herself into all kinds of trouble if she were any more obvious about her magical goings on.

It was her blatant disrespect for the rules that first caught his eye, however. She stood outside a candy shop in the small town of Belvidere, offering samples to anyone who wandered by. That in and of itself wasn't anything special, but the silent spell she wove with her fingers every time someone took a morsel that compelled them into the store was very special indeed. Anyone who watched from a distance could witness the fingers on her free hand twitching in mesmerizing patterns beneath the silver tray she held.

Her movements had caught his eye on his first day in town, ensnaring him. The next day, he walked around the town square hoping to catch another glimpse of her. By his third time around the square, she had emerged from the store with her tray, fingers dancing. It took stones to pull off magic like that out in the open, and Elech couldn't resist the draw of a woman with enough gumption to try it. He strode right up to the dark haired beauty and basked in the glow of her aura.

"Would you care to try a nut cluster?" Her voice was soft, breathy, and light. His stomach growled, full of a hunger that food would not satisfy.

"Don't mind if I do." He selected a chocolate from her tray, brought it to his nose for a tentative sniff, then popped it into his mouth. He could feel the impact of her spell as it collided with the explosion of chocolate and cashews mixed with a liquor of sorts on his tongue.

"Mmmm." He flashed her his most wicked smile and savored her offering. He nodded to her with a tip of his hat and began to walk away. "Good day."

"Sir? Wouldn't you care to go inside and purchase some more?" she called after him.

He turned back to her. "No. I think I've had just enough, witch. Unless you can offer me something a little more compelling to lure me in." He lifted his left hand and mimicked the motions of her fingers.

Her face paled and the hand holding the tray of chocolates shook. "I don't know what you're talking about." Her voice no longer held the sweet and innocent tone he'd come to identify with her in his short time watching her. Instead, it whipped at him, abrasive and full of accusation.

"Call me Elech. What do I call you?"

The woman made another sweeping gesture with her fingers, narrowed her eyes at him, and responded. "Cecily. Cecily Barren."

Elech moved to her, withdrew the tray from her hand, and set it on the open window's ledge.

"Well, Cecily, have I got a deal for you." He crooked a finger at her, beckoning her to follow him.

She eyed him, curiosity dancing behind her irises. He imagined her inner debate between following him or slapping his arrogant face and smiled wide. Wanting to weigh the conflict in his favor, he did what always seemed to intrigue a curious woman and flicked his dual tipped tongue between his lips with his most heady "come hither" stare.

"The deal expires in under a minute, Ma'am, so think quickly." He tipped his hat again and turned toward the park nestled in the square.

"Wait. I'll come with you."

Elech waited for her to catch up and, when she did, he slipped his arm around her waist and changed course leading her toward the Delaware River. The touch of his hands on her sparked a premonition of a baby. A girl. One who had his blood running through her veins. She was stunning with long dark locks of hair and Cecily's bright blue eyes. The scene in his mind shifted to one of the child, older somehow, standing before a large gate, one he swore he knew, that opened with only the touch of her hands. The woman in his vision reached toward him, offering her hand and admittance to this wondrous place. The place he had longed to belong, to bring to his father. He could see it plain as day. The Overworld would be his to hand deliver on a silver platter to his father. Or keep for himself…

To rule.

"So, you offered me a deal back there. What for?" she asked, tearing him away from the images playing out in his mind. They stopped at a bench that overlooked the river separating New Jersey from Pennsylvania and stood silent until the weight of the situation felt uncomfortable even on his shoulders.

"You are a witch, are you not?" he finally asked.

An almost imperceptible nod of her head was all she gave as an answer.

"Well, I'm a devil who needs a witch to help with a very personal situation." He studied her face and waited for the shock that he expected to come with his brutal honesty. In his two hundred years of searching, he had yet to admit to any of the women he bedded that he was anything more than a man, but today he felt adventurous.

She gazed out over the river and breathed deeply. "What kind of situation?"

The scent of spring in the air was intoxicating.

"I'd like to have an heir." He paused to let the implications of his words sink in. "And it seems a witch of your caliber would be strong enough to provide me one."

Cecily turned back to him and met his eyes. "What makes you think I'd even consider such a proposal?"

"A witch who has such little regard as to perform magic out in the open seems like one who might be agreeable to a night or two of passion, which I would be able to guarantee, of course." He leaned in close and tucked a strand of loose hair behind her ear. "Your passion would be my very first priority," he whispered. "And I can say I have had many lifetimes to perfect the art of pleasuring a woman." He appreciated the shiver that ran through Cecily's body, while her pupils dilated, and lips parted as his words hit their mark. He enjoyed knowing the heat of his words sank into her fully.

"Other than passion, what do I get out of this arrangement?" Once her breathing normalized and she regained control of her faculties, she still refused to meet his gaze.

"You would have the distinction as being the most powerful witch in the Northeast."

"I already hold that distinction," she countered.

"Ah, but to have snared a devil, that would give you more power than you can imagine."

She arched a brow and stared him down. "And how do I know you wouldn't dispose of me once the child was born?"

"Because I find you interesting—and that is not something I usually find humans to be." His honesty was making him feel soft, emotional, almost human, like his mother had been. He offered her a small smile and reached for her hand. "Besides, don't you want to know what it would be like to have a devil as your plaything? Yours to command? To control? I'm sure you understand the value in having such a thing in your witchy arsenal." He bowed at the waist, turned her hand in his, and touched his lips to the inside of her wrist.

"You are rather tempting," she agreed, her eyes fixated on his lips touching her skin.

"So say the words. Make it official. Come to me. For me." He pulled her close and inhaled the scent of her.

She whimpered and nodded her consent.

"Say it, witch. Say that you are mine."

"I'm yours," she whispered. "Is that what you needed to hear?" She moved close enough that he could smell the hint of chocolate on her breath. It was maddening, the sweetness that she offered coupled with the bite of contempt laced into her words.

"It is indeed." He closed the gap between them, capturing her lips in his. He was the first to break the embrace, but it wasn't for long. "I'm staying nearby. Come." The command rolled off his tongue with ease. Elech grabbed her hand and tugged her back toward the road.

Cecily stood firm, a hand on a hip, and a scowl

on her face. "Is that it? You just tell me to come and I'm to follow you? You do know that I have an opinion on the matter, right?"

Elech stared at the woman in disbelief. Never in all his years had a woman given him such difficulty. More often than not, he had more than his fair share of women offering to be at his beck and call. That was until one would wind up dead and he'd be forced to move along and start over, but that should have no bearing on the woman before him.

"I understand. The deal is not to your liking. So be it." He lifted his hat from his head and gave her a shallow bow before he replaced it and started toward the riverside cottage where he was staying. Not far down the road, he heard the sound of footsteps on the sidewalk behind him and a smile slid across his face. The witch had changed her mind. She would be his.

He continued on as if he didn't know she followed, but when he reached the porch of his temporary home, he unlocked the door and waited. Her gaze on his back caused a rush of heat over his skin. He turned to her saying not a word and awarded her with the smile he reserved only for his lovers.

Within minutes, he had her inside and undressed. For all her earlier objections, in the privacy of the cabin, she offered only one— anywhere but the bed. She muttered something about refusing to be like the others; as if she imagined long list of women in this place.

True to his word, he stayed far from the bedroom, instead choosing to take her in the sunlight that streamed through the back sitting room that over looked the river. He pinned her between his body and the crystal clear glass of the picture window. With nothing to keep her hidden from the view of any passersby, she came alive— writhing, moaning, wanton. It was the most intoxicating experience of his long life.

Each slide of his hands over her body called forth moans that rivaled the prayers sent by desperate humans into the ether. Panted breath fogged the glass pane as she pressed her exposed breasts against its coolness, pushing her perfectly rounded rear into his groin until his hardness had her begging for more.

Elech usually took great care with his women, worried their human frailty would be their undoing, but not with Cecily. She spurred him on with every screamed word that left her mouth and every greedy desire of her body, daring him to take her higher, harder, faster. She was insatiable. Shameless. And he basked in her need, traveling to new depths of his sexual prowess to give her all she demanded.

He had finally met his match. Sweat dripped off her body as he worked her into a frenzy of anticipation; waiting for that all-encompassing moment when he would take her over the edge and she would fly. As he drove into her, hands sliding across the glass pane of the window that overlooked the river, he whispered in her ear, "Come for me, witch. Give yourself to me. Now."

Cecily threw her head back, his name on her lips as her body tightened around him, and dragged him over the edge with her. Panting, they sank to the floor, their limbs entwined. Laying with her in his arms, Elech kept a close watch on her, waiting to see if her veins would turn black like all the other women he'd had before her. She smiled at him, contentment on her face as she mindlessly drew the shapes of ancient runes on his bare skin with her index finger. The life-affirming color never paled on her skin and her seductive caresses begged for his attention. Satisfaction rolled through him cresting like a wave on the shore as he pulled her astride him and took his pleasure again and again.

That evening when the sun slunk off to bed and the moon came out to play, Cecily rolled on her side and faced him with heavy lidded eyes.

"Promise me there won't be another until our child is born." She brushed his hair from his forehead. "Promise I will be all you need and that you will see to my needs without restraint."

"It's an easy promise to make." Elech wrapped her in his arms and pressed a kiss to her temple.

"How so?"

"You're the first woman to survive my mating. I'll keep you until you don't."

He rolled on top of her and pushed back into her depths. As long as she walked the earth, he wouldn't have need for another human.

Elech kept his promise until nine months later when Cecily, under the cover of darkness and social unwedded shame, delivered into his arms their son. While Elech stared into the eyes of his son, confusion in his mind, Cecily slipped away into the ether as she bled to death on the cot in a nunnery for unwed mothers. In that moment, Elech vowed to never think of her again. Not only had his premonition been wrong, but now fate had taken the one woman he had found that had the ability to provide him an heir and taken her from him.

The tiny child wiggled in his arms and his heart turned cold. There was no way he would raise this, this, thing. He handed the baby to the nursemaid and left with a promise that he'd keep an eye on the child from afar.

He would have his female heir if it took an eternity. All he needed was to keep an eye on the Barren boy he had left in the nunnery. Eventually, one of his heirs would birth a female and when they did, Elech would be waiting. He returned to his home, packed his belongings, and did what a devil was best at—he stole away under the cover of night and hid.

Watching.

Waiting.

Wanting.

TWO

1985

HIS WIFE'S SCREAMS bounced off the waiting room walls at the small rural hospital, and Donovan Barren sank further into his chair. His life was over. Nothing was more certain. *Nothing*.

A portly nurse with wild eyes and a yellow halo of untamed hair burst through the door that separated the waiting room from the birthing area. She scanned the room until her eyes met his.

"Mr. Barren, your wife is asking for you. It won't be long now until the babies come."

Donovan dropped his head into his hands and held back the flood of tears that threatened to spill. There was no way he was going to set a single foot into that room. It wasn't that he didn't love his wife; he did. It wasn't that he didn't adore the idea of having children; he did. It was that he already knew he had failed as a father. There was no disputing that fact. Especially considering that the New Jersey Devil sat beside him in the waiting room.

No one else seemed to notice the Devil's presence, yet everyone avoided a good ten-foot radius around them, like a force field somehow repelled the innocent from the unseen dark energy swirling, pulsing, beating, chilling everything it touched.

Donovan wished he could be ignorant like the rest of them, but he wasn't. He was cursed just like his father, and his father before him had been. Hell, the Barren's family tree had a Devil somewhere near the roots, so it wasn't as farfetched as it sounded to wind up cursed. As it was, this Devil had been the thirteenth child of a long ago witch, giving credence, Donovan thought, to the number being unlucky. Because in all reality there was nothing unluckier than being a direct descendant of a Devil. Especially this one.

Thirteen, as Donovan called the devil beside him, waited patiently with his hands clasped in his lap.

Growing up in New Jersey, everyone had heard the tale of the New Jersey Devil. They teased and taunted one another around campfires but they'd all lose sleep if they knew that the mysterious Jersey Devil wasn't as much of a fable as they thought.

"Mr. Barren?" The nurse eyed him, her head tilted at an angle that looked uncomfortable.

"Tell Hope I'll see her and the babies after they are born." A chill ran up his arm and settled in his spine as Thirteen slid a boney arm around his shoulder.

Judgment rippled off her in waves as she turned on her heel and marched back through the door.

"It won't be long now, Donnnnn-ovan," Thirteen purred in his ear. "Soon, I'll have exactly what you owe me for my charity."

"I don't owe you anything," he hissed under his breath. There was nothing worse than speaking with Thirteen than the odd glances of people who only saw a person talking to himself, because that was part of the curse Donovan carried with him. Unless the Devil decided otherwise, only he, and others cursed by Thirteen, could see him.

"Ahhhhh, but you do," Thirteen hissed. "If I recall, you were a naughty boy and naughty boys always pay for their deeds one way or another."

His vision went black and his brain conjured the image of a younger version of himself spying on Hope; spying because he knew he could no longer tolerate not having her for his very own. In his memory, she was young and beautiful with flowers in her hair. She danced in a freshly plowed cornfield, her skirt floating around her thighs in the warm fall breeze. A man appeared on a tractor further down the field and headed in her direction. The tractor stopped just before striking her. A yell escaped the man's mouth, his boot kicked at her shoulder, and her body fell to the ground. Rage had exploded in Donovan's chest. The memory of it called the pain right back to what was its rightful place, deep in his heart. He remembered every sure footstep he had taken, and the tightness of his grip when his hands had found purchase around the old man's neck.

But mostly he remembered the face of the farmer dying in his hands until the memory was replaced by the face of Thirteen. The laughing, smiling, smirking face that haunted his every waking minute. The very same smirk that Thirteen now wore.

He was right, of course. Donovan had coveted Hope and stolen her away from her abusive husband. Thirteen had been there waiting in the wind for him to make such a move. It was in his nature, he supposed, since he was one in a long line of men who had promised their souls for a chance at a better life. To keep his ass out of jail, and to bring Hope home with him to be his wife, had cost him his soul and his firstborn daughter.

It was the piece of the deal surrounding a daughter where Donovan thought he had Thirteen by the balls. He could live his life without a soul if it meant saving Hope but he never imagined there would be a child the devil could claim considering there had never been a female heir in his family's recorded history. All that changed, though, when Hope had gotten pregnant. The doctor had double-checked, and then triple checked, when he heard not one, not two, but three tiny beating hearts nestled in her body. Hope had been overjoyed by the prospect of triplets and declared that certainly one of the three would be a daughter; one that Hope would be able to dress up in lace and thread ribbons through her hair. The moment the words had left her mouth, Thirteen had appeared, hands clasped in glee. He would have his female after all. From that moment on, Donovan had dreaded this very minute.

Hope's screams echoed in his head until silence slammed against him in a rush of mixed emotion. The nurse poked her head out of the door and called, "Barren baby one is a boy." She then ducked back out of sight. Seven minutes later, her head once again appeared. "Barren baby two is a boy."

Donovan's heart jumped. Maybe Hope had been wrong. Maybe there wasn't a girl after all. Maybe Thirteen would have to be happy with just his battered soul at the end of it all, because there would never be another pregnancy. If he had to, he'd walk away from Hope and the kids and never look back if it saved them from owing a debt to Thirteen.

It was only because he glanced at his watch that Donovan knew his luck had run out. It was thirteen minutes past the hour when a resounding squealing baby cry rattled through the building like a trumpet sent from the ether. The nurse was back once more at the door.

"Barren baby three is a girl."

Thirteen disappeared without preamble once the words hit home, and Donovan did what he knew he could no longer avoid. His hands trembled and his footing was shaky as he followed the nurse into the massive birthing arena. Curtains hung from the ceiling on tracks to give the appearance of privacy, but the vastness of the room was almost too much to bear with the cries coming from every curtained section.

A voice he knew better than his own rose from the other side of the curtained area closest to the door. Hope. He hated that on today, the day their miracles joined the world of the living, he'd have to break her heart. It was the one thing he had vowed never to do since the moment he'd laid eyes on her years ago, but he no longer had a choice. Thirteen would come looking for their daughter. If not today, then another.

The nurse held a corner of the curtain back so he could duck through. His wife's brow glistened with sweat and her face was flushed, but the smile on her lips was broad and toothy as usual. Tucked in the crook of each arm was a tiny, porcelain-skinned bundle of mews both topped with downy wisps of charcoal-colored hair. But it was the squirming, shrieking, smallest bundle laid across her lap that commanded his immediate attention.

He reached down and laid a comforting hand on the baby's chest. The wiggling ceased and lashes thicker than the deepest forest flew open. Eyes the color of sapphires saw right into his soul.

"She's beautiful, isn't she?" Hope's voice pulled him out of his wonder-filled trance. "They all are, but she's so lively."

He looked at the two babies tucked safe in his wife's arms and had to agree. There was something special about the little wonder perched on Hope's lap. "She is beautiful. Just like her mother." It was true in many ways, but this baby was beautiful and not in the way that all new babies were in the eyes of their parents. No, this one was special. His gut clenched. It only made sense that this child would be so special. Thirteen had to have wanted her for a reason, but now that Donovan had laid eyes on all three of his children, he knew there was no way in hell he would hand them over. The Devil himself would have to crawl his way out of Hell and take them after going through him first.

Donovan gave his wife a sweet kiss on her forehead and lifted the sleeping boy from under her right arm. "Which one is he?"

"He's the middle child. He gave us a bit of a scare. The doctor thought he might be breech, but it turned out he was just being stubborn."

"What should we name him?" Donovan stared at his son sleeping peacefully in his arms. He was the biggest of the three babies, and with the fight he'd given the doctor, he needed a good, solid name.

"I figured we'd keep with the tradition of D names for the boys. I know that was important to your father," Hope answered as she shifted his other son into a more comfortable position, all the while trying not to jostle their daughter.

"No. The name thing hasn't brought anything but misery to my family. I refuse to carry on a tradition that makes me feel bound to a man who sold us out."

"Darling, your father did the best he could, and look at us now. You have a successful real estate business, we have a nice home and three beautiful babies to fill it with."

Words caught in his throat. Hope had no idea that he'd paid dearly for his success. For her. So much so, that when the day came, he would be minus one soul and spending eternity in the only place people feared more than Newark: Hell.

"I was thinking we should name this little guy Dax," Hope continued, "and this little one reminds me of a Dominic. I'm not sure why, but it just feels right for him."

"Hope, really, we don't need D names. Anything would be fine: Jack, Anthony, Sylvester, anything."

"Donny, I picked them out a long time ago. I was going to go with Daniel for baby three, but that won't work now. Maybe Daniella?" Hope's nose wrinkled like the name tasted bad on her tongue.

"No. Not Daniella. She needs, I don't know, something more." He set Dax down in a waiting bassinet and lifted his daughter. A little fist worked its way free from the confines of the blanket swaddled around her, and her eyes peered up at him. "Daphne. We should name her Daphne." The little girl's eyes sparked with understanding. It couldn't be. She was barely an hour old and there was no way she could understand this moment, but still those stunning eyes twinkled at him like they were the only two people in the world.

"That's a beautiful name for her, Donny. Daphne. I love it." The baby at Hope's side squirmed and a cry louder than Donovan thought was possible for something so small to make erupted from its mouth. "Oh, is Dominic hungry? Momma will feed you, sweet boy."

Donovan watched his wife feed their child and a feeling of peace settled over him. He laid Daphne in a bassinet and moved a plastic chair between the two babies. He perched there between them, like a sentry on patrol. Silently, he vowed to each of his children that as long as he lived nothing would ever harm them. He swore to them a silent oath that he would never let Thirteen get his hands on them, nor their souls. He would teach them to be content and not to want what wasn't theirs. He'd teach them patience and respect. He'd teach them that pricy things were only that, things, and that they didn't bring the happiness that one hoped. He'd teach them to be fearful of strangers offering gifts. But most of all, he'd teach them to never underestimate the power of the Devil.

THREE

HOPE AND ALL three babies drifted off to sleep leaving Donovan with nothing to do other than watch the synchronized rise and fall of three tiny chests. A nurse had offered to send the babies off to the nursery, but he'd refused. There was no way he was letting them out of his sight. He had already mastered the art of diapering, swaddling, and burping.

While he stared at the miracle that was his daughter, a chill crept over his skin. Donovan leapt from his seat and braced his body over the bassinet holding her.

"Sillll-y fool. A promise is a promise." Thirteen tsked, shook his head, and approached Dax. "He will be a strapping young man some day. I can see it now. He will come to hate you for what you will do to his sister and will join me without hesitation."

Pain flooded Donovan's heart. Thirteen was trying

to make him lose his focus so he could take Daphne. Resolve tore through the pain and held him steady as he hovered over his little girl. The chill intensified with Thirteen's approach.

Thirteen peered into Dominic's bassinet. "Ah, this one is doomed to love another's beloved just like his father. Easy pickings he will be for sure, but we both know they are nothing compared to Daphne."

Donovan whipped around, arms up, ready for a fight. "Don't you dare say her name," he ground the words between clenched teeth. "She will never be yours. I will do whatever it takes to keep her from knowing you even exist."

"Donny? Who are you talking to?" Hope's voice, thick from slumber, pulled him from his standoff.

"Tell her, Donnnnn-ovan. She deserves to know." Thirteen raised a hand in mock salute and his tongue flicked past the edge of his teeth.

"Damn you to hell!" Donovan cried when the Devil moved close enough to flick his tongue over Hope's cheek.

"Donny, you're scaring me," she whispered. "Please tell me what's going on." Her pleas weighed on what little of his soul he could still claim as his own.

Thirteen bent low, inhaled the scent of Hope's hair, and sighed. His eyes disappeared beneath his eyelids as a sigh escaped his lips. "She was worth it, wasn't she, Donnnnn-ovan? She smells like heaven. Too bad she won't be yours much longer." The sneer on his face was downright unholy. "I'll return and then we will settle your debt." A nod of the head punctuated the promised threat as Thirteen disappeared as quickly as he had come.

Donovan raced to his wife's side, grabbed her in his arms, and held her tight against his chest. "Oh, Hope, please forgive me. I've done a horrible thing and I don't know how to fix it." Tears rolled freely down his cheeks in heated rivers and pooled on his beloved wife's chest. He buried himself in her warm embrace and cherished the feel of her small hands on his shoulders.

"Donny, whatever it is, we'll get through it together," she cooed in his ear and patted his back. "It's okay, Donny. It's okay."

He remained there, nestled in her embrace until the last of his sobs died away and the tears dried up. He glanced over at the three bassinets and dreaded the words he had to say. He cursed his forefathers for somehow creating this damn situation with the devil in the first place. The men in his family had all been weak-willed and susceptible to Thirteen's charms. That would end, here and now, with him. He would offer Thirteen his life today so his children could be spared.

He sat on the edge of the bed and clasped Hope's hands in his. "Do you remember the day we met?"

She gave him an odd look. "Of course I remember. You came to my family's farm stand and bought every last apple that was for sale." She laughed at the memory.

"What if I told you that wasn't the first time we met?"

She slid her hands from his grasp. "What are you talking about? I remember that day like it was yesterday. Are you feeling alright?"

"I should've told you this before, but I just wanted you to have the good memories of us." He paused to gather his thoughts and stared at the blank wall of the small private hospital room. "We met in town at the grocery store months before I came to the farm. I was standing in the produce aisle trying to pick a good melon and you helped me. You were beautiful, and kind, and had a smile that would make any grown man take notice of your beauty."

He took a breath and forced the words out. "I didn't know you were married. That didn't come out until much later, after I'd talked you into meeting me for quiet lunches and dates in the park. Your father had sold you off with the farm to some asshole that was beating you. I remember the first time I saw the handprint bruise on your neck. You begged me to forget about it, and you, but I couldn't. In all my life I had never known someone so pure and good as you, and even though you refused to see me, I was consumed with thoughts of you. I bought a track of land across from your farm so I would have an excuse to see you. And then, one warm fall day, there you were. You were dancing at the edge of the cornfield near the produce stand. I remember seeing a flash of pale blue panties from under your dress when the wind kicked up your skirt. It was as if even the wind taunted me with what I couldn't have."

"No," she whispered. "I wasn't married before. My father had the farm for sale when I met you. It sold soon after we started dating. He put the money into my trust, remember?" she begged, pulling herself up into a seated position on the hospital bed.

Donovan wished he could take the words back and let her live with the memory she had, but he'd already come this far and once he uttered the words, the spell holding her memory captive would dissolve leaving her with the bitter truth.

"Hope, please let me finish." He choked out the words. "Your husband caught me looking at you. He thought you were showing off for me even though you didn't know I was there. He kicked you to the ground and was about to hurt you, and I couldn't let him do that anymore. So I did what I had to do." His voice trailed off leaving them both sitting in the silence of the room.

"What did you do?" The whispered words plucked at his heartstrings.

"I killed him. I killed the bastard that was beating you and then I made a deal with a devil to erase your memory of it and make you mine. As long as I never told you about your past, those memories would live dormant in your mind; untouchable." His heart broke as the words left his mouth in a torrent. What had he done? He'd sold his soul for a lifetime of happiness with this woman and now here he was telling her all of his sins and hoping that somewhere in that kind, gentle heart of hers she would be able to forgive him.

"No." The word barely seeped through her lips. "No. It can't be true." She grabbed his face and forced him to meet her eyes.

What he saw there, in her gaze, crushed every hopeful fiber of his being. There was no coming back from this now. There was nothing he could do to repair the damage he had just caused.

"I'm sorry, Hope. I'm so, so sorry." He watched as pain rolled across her face, visible evidence of the memories returning with a vengeance. He had wanted to spare her from this, but the reality was she needed to know if she was going to be able to keep their children safe.

"It's true. Every word you said was true." A wild look flashed in her eyes. "Oh my God, I was married. His name was Edgar. He beat me when he drank and he raped me while I slept." She pulled her legs in tight against her chest and wrapped her arms around them.

Before his very eyes, Donovan watched all the joy eek out of his wife's body. She shrank in on herself until she was merely a shell of the vibrant woman he loved and adored. He was no better than the asshole that had beaten her. Damn it, he was worse because he had bargained for the false memories to protect her and then yanked them away when she was at her most vulnerable. And the worst was still to come because he had to tell her the terms of his deal with Thirteen. She had to know because if he couldn't get Thirteen to renegotiate, he'd need Hope to be strong enough to take the kids and run; run far from him and never look back.

FOUR

THIRTEEN YEARS LATER...

ON DAYS LIKE today when the cold wind blew over the mountains and cooled the autumn air, Donovan had to work hard to remember that life was not as it appeared. There was nothing quiet and calm about the life his family led. Not really.

He sat on the back porch and watched Hope hang sheets on the clothesline. It still amazed him that she was here, with him, and, every day he woke with her by his side, he thanked whatever sliver of luck that still held out. Daphne, Dax, and Dominic hooted and hollered from the woods surrounding the house where they played without a care in the world. He envied their ability to be carefree and oblivious. It was a luxury neither he, nor Hope, had. Instead they lived hidden away in a house near the top of a mountain in the town of Harmony, New Jersey always looking over their shoulder.

As far as census data went, it was a quaint town with more cows than people. Their neighbors were far away and few in number. Although the laughter of his children echoed around the mountain and bounced off the bare trees, he was almost certain that no one for miles knew that children lived here. The triplets often begged to go into town and play with other children, but after so many years of hearing "No," they stopped asking and resigned themselves to being the odd children of recluse parents. They studied hard with Hope as their teacher, and Donovan worked in real estate again, this time as a lowly agent. The funds from the sale of his business back near the shore, and Hope's trust account, got them through years of moving, hiding, and playing keep-away from Thirteen.

While the kids lived in a state of constant oblivion as to why their parents kept them so isolated, he and Hope worried constantly that today would be the day the devil came knocking. It wasn't like they hadn't tried to move farther away or escape to another part of the country, but ever since the day of the children's birth, any time Donovan got close to the physical border of the state, he would come down in a fit of excruciating pain. One time he begged Hope to just take the kids and leave him behind. He refused to hear where she planned to go so that when asked, he could honestly be ignorant of their whereabouts. But Hope's attempt at leaving the state was as unsuccessful as his. Only it wasn't her who suffered; it was the kids. They came down with simultaneous headaches that rivaled the worst migraines and stomachaches that they collectively compared to their stomach's being twisted into tight knots reserved for ropes that anchored ships at docks.

So they ticked off day after day on the calendar

and waited. For what, they weren't entirely sure, but it didn't stop them from the task. Every morning Donovan would wake before the family and pour a steady stream of salt around the perimeter of the property. Then, he'd set the house temperature just warm enough that a chill would be easily detected on his skin if Thirteen broke through the salt barrier. Before he left the house for work, he'd check the salt again, fixing any spots that looked like they needed fortification. He'd then prick a finger with a tie pin that had been handed down from his grandfather, after a witch had recommended the use of blood to ward off their devilish ancestor years ago, and draw the sign of a guardian angel with his blood in the dirt at the edge of the front yard.

Over the years he and Hope had researched the occult and he'd begun making trips into Belvidere to The Daily Dews, an occult bookstore, newspaper stand, and coffee shop. The store had been in the hands of a local family for decades and the older couple that ran it were self-proclaimed wiccans. Ten years before he met them, their daughter and her husband had been killed by what was thought to be a bear while they were out in the woods participating in a solstice ceremony. The Dewsberrys weren't so certain that the attack had been a bear, but in a place so far removed from the everyday niceties, there wasn't a lot you could do to dispute such a vicious attack. Instead, they raised their granddaughter and peddled their merchandise.

When Donovan had first noticed the store, he'd gone out of his way to avoid it, and the shopkeepers, out of what he thought of as a 'respectful fear.' Given his upbringing and personal experience with Thirteen, where the word occult could be found, the devil couldn't be far behind.

That was until he bumped into Mrs. Dewsberry at the corner deli one day at lunchtime. She teased that he looked like the devil had made him jump out of his skin, and when he didn't laugh with her, she had pulled him aside and whispered in his ear. The whispered words rattled him to the core. She knew all about Thirteen; knew he was more than a story kids told around campfires to scare one another. She hadn't seen him herself, but that was only because the cloak of her family's white magic that kept her, and the block surrounding The Daily Dews, from the devil's purview. After that day, Donovan made an effort to stop into the Dews and chat with the couple. They were the one's who had recommended the salt and taught him the sign of the guardian angel.

Hope often asked if she could invite the Dewsberrys for dinner so that the children could have a friend, but Donovan always discounted the idea saying that as much as he liked them, he couldn't be certain it wouldn't put them in danger too. Days passed and melted into months, which ticked along into years, and now they were a week away from the triplet's thirteenth birthday.

When he wasn't at work and able to watch the kids, Hope ran around town picking out the perfect gifts for their soon-to-be-teenagers, selecting decorations that would suit them all. Donovan didn't take much joy in the upcoming celebration, however. Instead, he sat and watched the children and prayed to anyone that might be listening in heaven above to keep them safe, because in the very back of his mind, the thought of their thirteenth birthday nagged at what little remained of his soul. He found himself unable to keep the kids out of his sight for long as the day drew ever closer.

The first snow of the season sent the entire family outside.

"Dad. Come on. Join us," Dax hollered.

Donovan smiled and waved to his son. "Nah, I'll sit here and watch you guys have fun," he called back.

"Daaaaaad," whined Daphne. "I'm not a guy!"

"I never said you were, princess," he reassured.

"Ugh, her head's gonna get too fat for her neck," Dax complained.

Nic joined in with, "You mean it isn't already?"

"Do you hear how they talk to me, Daddy?"

From his spot on the porch, Donovan watched her lashes flutter under the weight of the first few flakes of snow that fell. That girl would eventually be the death of him. If it wasn't because of his deal with the devil, it would be because some poor sap fell hard for her beauty and charms.

"Boys, leave your sister alone," Hope rebuffed while she wrestled with the sheets dancing in the wind that she had forgotten on the clothesline the night before. "You know it's not nice to pick on a girl."

"But mom, she's one of us," Dax argued. "Even if she is growing boobs." He stuck his tongue out at his sister, then dodged to catch a falling flake on it.

"Gross. Seriously, you two are sooooo immature." Nic contorted his face in disgust and pretended to throw up.

"Get over yourself, Nic. You aren't that much older than we are," Daphne countered to her oldest brother. "Besides, don't think we don't know you still sleep with that blanket mom made for you."

"Oh, now you're gonna get it," Nic yelled, running through the underbrush toward his sister.

Leaves flew into the air as the kids yelled and chased one another. Hope set the basket of laundry under the cover of the porch roof, removed her gloves, and settled on the chair beside Donovan. "They're something, aren't they?"

"Yes they are. It's hard to believe they're almost teenagers. Soon they'll be wanting to learn how to drive."

"You know we can't keep them cooped up here forever, right?"

It was the beginning of a very old argument; one that he'd been on the winning side of each and every time, but today he could feel the winds of change in the air. Hope wasn't going to keep backing down. That was the price he'd have to pay for their comfort. It'd been close to eight years that they'd lived here and stopped running with every bad feeling, and over those eight years Hope had gotten less worried. Memories of her old life once again faded into the background, and she had found ways to be happy mothering, teaching, and loving their kids.

It never stopped amazing him that despite everything he'd done to cause them so much trouble, she still loved him. The spark they'd shared early in their relationship had faded, as he assumed it did in most marriages, but still she held his hands and kissed his lips, and he never once questioned her love. He hadn't questioned since the day they had run from the hospital, triplets in hand.

"We've been over this a thousand times." He didn't have a better answer for her. Instead he shook his head and went back to watching the kids play.

"Donny, I've been so lonely here. Imagine what it'd be like for them to actually have friends; for us to have friends." She slid her hand to his knee, and when he finally met her eyes, she dropped to the ground at his feet. Her hands slid on the outside of his legs until she hit the bottom of the middle of his thigh. With a quick glance over her shoulder at the kids who were running about through the trees, she slid her fingers over the denim to the apex of his legs. She was playing dirty this time. With three almost-teens in the house, moments like this, intimate and clandestine, were few and far between.

"Hope. Stop. The kids…"

"Are playing. And so am I." A perfectly sculpted eyebrow raised, capping off the wicked gleam in her eye. "Now, don't you think we'd all benefit from a little fun? You can invite the Dewsberrys over and if all goes well, maybe we can actually find someone we trust with the kids for long enough that we can get a few hours to ourselves." She leaned in close, her fingers snaking their way along the zipper of his jeans until she held the tab between her fingers. She slid it down one torturous tooth at a time, prickling his nerve endings with every bit of flesh that became exposed to the cold air.

When the very tips of her fingers brushed along his sensitive skin, he clamped a hand over hers and gave her an amused look. "Alright. You win. I'll go give them a call." Donovan slid his zipper back into place, retreated into the house and leaned against the cold, hard granite until the coolness of it shook him free from his heated thoughts. If there was anything he could do to keep Hope happy, he would, and if it just so happened to end with her making him happy, all the better.

FIVE

A WEEK LATER, Donovan found himself sitting at a cleared picnic table in his backyard with the Dewsberrys. Their granddaughter, Calliope, and Daphne warmed themselves by the fire while the boys winged snowballs at one another from behind walls of snow. Hope bustled about carrying leftovers back into the house with Mrs. Dewsberry in her wake while her husband, Stan, sat watching the boys.

"You have quite the family here, Donovan. I never knew you had kids, much less triplets," Stan ventured.

"Well, Hope and I are pretty private people," he countered.

"It's just odd that we've known yous guys for so long and never knew about your kids." Stan's Jersey lilt shone through in his words as he tilted his head and studied the girls who were shaping their own secret stash of snowballs behind where they sat.

"I guess it just never came up." Even to his own ears, the excuse sounded weak.

"All that talk about 'you-know-who' and 'you-know-what' and you never mentioned them. Do they even know?"

"Look, Mr. Dewsberry..."

"Stan. Call me Stan. After all the time you've spent coming around, you should start calling me by my first name," the man interrupted.

"Stan," Donovan continued. "It's not your business how we raise our kids. Hope and I are keeping them safe and we'll continue to do so. They don't have anything to worry about when it comes to Thirteen and my 'you-know-what'." He hoped the stern look he sent Stan's way hit home and ended the conversation.

"I don't think it's right not to tell them. If you're cursed, then so are they. Don't cha think they have the right to know?"

"No. I don't." Arguing was a moot point, but Donovan couldn't let it go that easily. "I'm cursed, but they aren't; at least not yet. Remember, my family is a direct damn line of descendants from the Devil himself. I'll give anything to keep those kids from his clutches, to keep them from ending up like me. As long as we can keep them from needing his help, there will be no reason for them to sell their souls. So I'll do whatever it takes. Anything."

"What else do you have to give? He already has the right to your soul."

"Look Stan, you don't know shit about this. I beg your pardon for my crass language, but this isn't something I want to discuss. Not now. *Not ever*. Okay?"

The older gentleman nodded. "Whatever you say." He pulled his coat closer around his body and walked off.

When the evening stars began to light the sky, Donovan lit the yard torches. Daphne and Calliope took turns braiding one another's hair by the warmth of the fire pit while Nic strummed his guitar. Dax grabbed an almost empty jug of pool filter sand and turned it over to drum on. In minutes, the two had a nice tune going and everyone stopped what they were doing to listen.

Calliope moved to sit beside Dax, scooped a handful of sand from the frozen ground, and dropped it into an empty plastic cup. She caught the beat and added the sound of a shaker to the tune. When she opened her mouth and began to sing, everything else around them stopped. The boys stopped playing, the night owls stopped squawking; even the night breeze stopped blowing, all waiting to hear the beautiful song pouring from the young girl's mouth.

Dax was the first to break out of the trance and pick up the beat, but Nic sat open-mouthed as he stared at the girl across from him. Donovan knew the look on his son's face all too well. He remembered having that same look himself the first time he had laid eyes on Hope. This should be a joyous occasion; his children making a new friend and his oldest meeting his first crush. Their thirteenth birthday had gone off without a hitch and, as far as he was concerned, today was everything a typical day should be for the kids, but he knew it couldn't be so.

Nic finally picked his jaw off the ground enough to grip his guitar and join in with his brother and Calliope.

"Did you see that, Donny? I think Dax has a thing for Callie." Hope stood behind him and wrapped her arms around him, snuggling into his warmth.

"Dax? No, I must've missed that." He studied his middle child banging on the empty drum and swaying with the beat.

"Yeah, he's been trying to get her to notice him all day," she whispered in his ear. "They'd make a lovely couple. Don't you think?"

"Hon, they're only thirteen. Calliope's even younger. It's a little premature to be pairing them off. Besides, I think Nic might give Dax a run for his money. Didn't you see his jaw hit the floor when she started singing?" He guided Hope around to meet her eyes and pulled her onto his lap.

"Oh, that was just him being surprised I think," she offered, a coy smile tugging at her lips.

"I don't know," he started to say, but stopped. It wasn't in his nature to argue unnecessarily with Hope, and this was one of those times it would be to his benefit to leave it alone. He reserved his arguments for the ones that their lives depended on.

"I think Callie is going to grow to be a beautiful young woman and then Stan and Lisa will have their hands full."

"Just like we will have with Daphne," he added.

"Not if you keep her locked away far from the prying eyes of society." Hope protested and nibbled on his jawline under the cover of the shadows created by the night sky. "By the time she's climbed over this threshold it will be over your dead body, and she'll be too old and tired to bother."

"Sounds perfect to a father's ears." His laughter came easily for the first time in so long that it damn near made him jump.

By eleven, the kids were running low on energy and all the adults were past their limit without the aide of caffeine. The adults took on the tasks of cleaning up and putting the fire out while the kids pledged to repeat the day again soon. It broke Donovan's heart to watch his children holding on to the hope that maybe today something had changed enough that they would be able to have regular friendships, because he knew the truth was they'd never be able to be 'normal' kids.

"It was great seeing you all," Lisa called and waved before she slid into the front seat. Stan offered a wave and started the car.

Calliope was a different story, though. Donovan watched as she and Daphne wrapped their arms around each other and hugged as if supernatural forces were tugging at them. Not to be outdone, Dax went in for a similar hug and finished with tickling the girl's ribs so that she wiggled against him. Sly kid. Donovan was certain Dax knew what he was doing. Though it was Nic he watched interact with Calliope most intently.

Nic offered a hand but Calliope threw her arms around him in a bear hug. In typical Nic fashion he lifted her off the ground and placed a sweet kiss on the top of her blonde head. The girl gave him the most curious look before she went in for a second hug. The look on Nic's face was pure heaven, but Dax's was a mix of twisted emotions.

In the red glow of brake lights, Donovan's eyes were drawn to a shadow at the edge of the property. His heartbeat stuttered for a beat then catapulted into action.

"Inside. Now." His tone was hard and unforgiving.

"But Daddy," Daphne whined.

"Now. Don't make me say it again," he warned. He caught Hope's eyes and nodded over his shoulder. She wouldn't be able to see Thirteen standing at the edge of their driveway, but she'd trust that he did.

"Come on kids, it's late." She wrapped an arm around Daphne's waist and leaned in close enough to whisper something in her ear while herding her into the house. Dax and Nic followed behind, but not until Dax had given his dad a strange look; a look that may not have even been aimed at him. Could it be that his son saw the shadow of the devil standing just outside the salted line of defense? Donovan shook the thought from his mind and followed his family inside.

Hope hustled the kids off to bed and busied herself in the kitchen until Donovan turned the deadbolt on the back door.

"Was it him? Is he out there?" Fear dripped off every syllable and her hands stilled midway in their journey from the sink to the towel on the oven door. Water dripped into a small pool on the floor beside her feet, unnoticed.

"Yes."

"Why is he here now?" Her hands wiped across her jeans and she moved to his side.

"I'm not sure. Maybe because we opened our home to others?"

"Donny," she whimpered. "It couldn't have been that. We've been so careful, and you said that Lisa has some way of blocking him from seeing her family. Right?"

"She said something about that, but maybe it only works at the Dews. I don't know, but I'm sure it was him out there." He wrapped his arms around his wife and sought comfort in the feel of her body pressed against his. He wasn't going to let Thirteen take this moment away from his family. They were all happy and finally had some semblance of normalcy in their lives. Anger bubbled into rage in the pit of his stomach. If there was a last straw in a feud with the Devil this was it.

He set Hope back from his grasp and wrapped a scarf around his neck. "I'm going to go deal with him. If I don't come back, take the kids and go."

"Donny, you're scaring me." Hope's eyes blazed and she grabbed for his retreating form. "I won't leave without you."

Donovan stopped abruptly, sending his wife careening into his back. He turned and met her worried eyes with an icy stare. It landed with his desired effect because she stepped back and shuddered. He'd often watched it happen between his parents as he grew up and knew that, for the first time in their lifetime, Hope saw the soullessness within him. The darkness rose to the surface with his ire. It broke his heart to see the terrified look on Hope's beautiful face, but he needed her to follow his orders. It was the only chance he had at saving them if Thirteen chose to enact revenge on him for what he was about to do.

"Say it. Say you'll take the kids and leave if I'm not back in fifteen minutes." His voice was as cold as the night air.

"I'll leave. I'll take the kids somewhere safe," she whispered, but she couldn't bring her eyes to meet his.

He placed a finger under her chin to draw her eyes up to meet his. "I need you to know that I always loved you. From the first moment I saw you, I knew I'd do anything to have you as my own, and I've never regretted that. Not even when he ripped my soul from my body. Not even when he threatened to take the kids the day they were born. But, if something happens to me and you don't take them and run, I will never forgive you."

He knew his tone would shame her into compliance and it sickened him that he used her abusive past as a weapon to control her in this moment, but he was desperate. And desperate men did desperate things. That's how he found himself in this situation in the first place.

SIX

DONOVAN DIDN'T LOOK back when he left the warmth of his home and trudged down the porch steps to face the Devil. He wished he had grabbed his coat. The cold drilled through his flannel shirt and bore straight through to his bones with painful accuracy the nearer he came to where Thirteen stood.

"Donnnnn-ovan. I've waited a long time for this day." Thirteen stood in the night, strong and solid in the cold surrounding him. He looked the same as always, never seeming to age past his mid-twenties, never maturing into old age. Unlike the talks of the Jersey Devil's inhumane appearance, Thirteen stood on two legs like any man. He wore suits like any door-to-door salesman might, and his eyes showed no signs of a red glow. In fact, the only thing that stood out as inhuman about him was the forked tongue that caused a slight lisp when he spoke.

"You can just keep waiting." Donovan's bravado surprised even him. Who would have thought that in the face of this much evil, he could actually show a spine instead of being the coward he'd always been. Pride welled in his gut and a surge of strength shot through his body. He could do this. He could refuse the devil and send him on his way. He *would* do this.

"The silly boy has become a silly man."

Donovan watched as Thirteen neared the barrier of salt and his breath stalled in his throat.

"Did you think this would keep me from collecting my payment?" He pointed a long, spindly finger at the ground. "That might work for witches. Maybe even demons." His lips parted in a sinister smile that sent a chill down Donovan's spine. "But I'm immune to salt Donnnnn-ovan." With that, Thirteen stepped over the salt line.

Donovan's pulse dropped. Whatever power he thought he'd had moments ago was gone and he was the same scared man he'd been years ago when Thirteen had first whispered in his ear. He looked over his shoulder, desperate for Hope and the kids to still be safely behind the door of their home.

"The girl will be mine. It's only a matter of time," Thirteen hissed.

"I won't let you take her. Take me instead," Donovan begged, but the devil kept moving forward. "I'll let you take me. Right now. Just leave my family alone," he beseeched.

"I already have you, or have you forgotten?"

Thirteen cocked his head to the side and studied him.

"But you can take *my* life. With the end of my life, my soul will fully be yours. Isn't that the way this works? You have my soul in name only now. You can't use it until I die. Kill me. Just leave them alone."

"Why would I kill you, Donnnnn-ovan? With you alive I can get so much more out of you." The smile on the devil's face in that moment would haunt him forever.

"What do you want?" He moved to put himself between the house and the monster moving steadily closer with every passing beat of his heart. "I'll do anything. *Anything*." Donovan dropped to his knees and bowed his head. He knew the sound of defeat in his voice would get Thirteen's attention. Desperation was like a drug to a being like Thirteen. He bathed in it and drank in the hopelessness of mere mortals. The creak of the front door sounded behind him. His time was growing to a close if he was going to be able to save his family. He reached forward and clasped the devil's feet. "I'll do *anything* you ask."

"Anything? Silly man. You have no idea what you offer." A cold hand ruffled his hair like he was a small child. "Bring me a pure soul, and I'll give you an extension."

Donovan met his dark eyes. "A what?"

"A soul that is pure of heart. One that will give themselves to me willingly." Thirteen steepled his fingers together, anticipation lighting his face.

"How do I find someone willing to give their soul to you for nothing in return?" Dread crept over his nerve endings and swirled his bloodstream. This was a ruse. No one would ever volunteer to give their soul to the devil.

"Ah, that's a special challenge that you have exactly forty-eight hours to overcome." Thirteen's boney fingers dug into Donovan's hair and pulled until he had no choice but to meet his deadly gaze. "If you don't, I'll be back. And this time I'll leave with your soul *and* your daughter, plus the promises of the souls of both your sons." A dry laugh escaped his thin lips. "Do you understand?" He tilted his head and pulled his eyes away from Donovan's. His tongue flicked between his lips like a snake readying himself to strike. "Ah, your failure will give me so much pleasssss-ure."

A chill wracked Donovan's body and left a dark emptiness inside of him. Before he could say another word, Thirteen was gone and the snow on the ground beneath him had soaked through his jeans.

The crunch of snow behind him spurred his body into motion while his brain played a game of catch-up. He sprang to his feet and whirled around before he could feel the next beat of his heart, his hands wrapping around the throat of the being behind him. With every ounce of strength in his body he held fast and squeezed.

It wasn't until the soft sputter reached his ears that he realized it was Hope struggling for breath beneath his fingers, not Thirteen. He released his hands and dropped to the ground with her. She coughed and struggled for breath and all he could do was watch helplessly. He didn't dare touch her.

He didn't dare do anything but pray beneath his breath. How could he have been so careless?

When her body stopped struggling for breath and she relaxed back onto her haunches, he dared to meet her eyes. Regret stabbed him right in the heart. What he saw in her eyes was worse than any funhouse mirror. Where he'd always seen patience, love, and devotion, he now saw hurt, anger, and distrust.

"Hope," he started.

"Don't." She cut him with a look and rose to her feet. He watched the roll of emotions wash over her face as she transformed from the hurt victim into the strong woman he knew and adored. "Don't say anything. There is no excuse for what you did. You wanted the kids and me gone, right? Well, we're going." She turned from him and headed back to the house.

Whispered words left his lips. "Wait. Please."

She stopped but refused to turn around.

"Sorry won't be enough. I know that. But please don't leave. You and the kids aren't safe."

She swung around and leveled a steely gaze at his chest, seemingly unable to meet his eyes. "I've stood beside you for fifteen years. I've given you three beautiful children. I've packed them up in the night and run at your insistence, and through it all I've never doubted that you loved me or had our best interests at the forefront of your mind." Her words overflowed the tears in her eyes, sending dueling rivers down her cheeks. "Until tonight. I think you are a very sick man, Donovan Barren.

You need help." She turned and walked back toward the house.

"Hope, please. Listen to me. He was here and he wants Daphne. I thought you were him. I'm trying to protect you. Hope…" Her name caught in his throat. She shut the door behind her and he heard the click of the deadbolt.

Cold minutes passed and bled into one another. He hadn't moved from his spot in the yard, watching the figures of his family moving behind the curtains covering the windows, until one by one the lights behind the curtains blinked out. The last to go was the porch light, leaving him in complete darkness. A few minutes later the front door creaked open and Nic took a tentative step through the door.

Donovan raced to the porch. There was no telling if Thirteen was still lurking in the shadows waiting for an opportunity to snatch one of them. "What are you doing out here in the cold, buddy?"

"Dad." He wrapped his arms around Donovan's midsection and held tight.

"It's okay, buddy," Donovan reassured, patting his back. "You shouldn't be out here."

"Why is mom so upset? And why are you out here all by yourself? Who was that man you were talking to?"

Donovan's blood ran cold. He pried Nic from his hold and pushed him an arm's length away. "What did you say?"

"I asked why mom's so upset." His young face

was clouded by emotion.

"Not about mom, Nic. About the man?"

"Who is he?"

"Was this the first time you've seen him?" Donovan bent to meet his son's tired eyes. "Tell me. Has he been here before?" When his son didn't answer him right away, he grabbed his shoulders and gave him a little shake. "Nic. I need to know if you've seen him before."

Nic dropped his gaze to his slipper-clad feet. "Sometimes we see him in the woods when we play."

"Tell me you haven't spoken to him," Donovan cried. "Tell me you haven't."

"No, Sir. I haven't talked to him."

Nic's downcast eyes told a different story, so Donovan continued, "What about your brother and sister? Have they?"

Nic shuffled his feet and tried to pull out of his grasp.

"Please, son. Tell me the truth. It's important. I need to know if that man's spoken with your brother or sister."

"Is he your dad?" Nic's voice was low and his questioning eyes finally met his father's.

The question caught Donovan off guard. "Why do you ask that? What did he say?" Thoughts raced in his head as he tried to figure out Thirteen's angle.

"He said he was our long-lost grandfather." Nic kicked the toe of his slipper into the back of his other heel. It was the tic that meant there was more to the story than he felt comfortable telling.

Donovan sat on the porch steps, deflated and vulnerable. "What else did he tell you? I'm sure he had more to say than that. It's okay to tell me, Nic. I won't be upset. I promise."

"But you got upset with mom. We saw you."

"I wasn't upset with your mother. I was upset with the man and thought it was him behind me. I didn't want him to hurt you guys." Donovan ran a hand through his hair. What did Thirteen have to gain by lying to the kids? "It's okay Nic, tell me."

"He told us if there was anything we ever needed all we had to do was ask and he'd take care of us, because he knew there would be a day that we'd need him to help with something you couldn't." Nic dropped to the ground and scooted beside him. "I didn't talk to him, Dad, I swear, but Dax asked what kind of things he could help with. The man told him he could do anything our heart wanted. He said he helped you get away with murder but we didn't believe him and we ran back to the house."

"What about your sister? Was she there?"

"No, but I think she's seen him too. I've seen her talking to herself outside. Kinda like he's there but we can't see him."

The bottom of Donovan's stomach clenched and fell. He was going to be sick; there was no stopping it. He sprang to the railing and leaned over just in time to empty the contents of his stomach onto the snow-covered garden below. The kids shouldn't be able to see Thirteen if their souls were still intact. Something had gone terribly wrong.

SEVEN

THE NEXT MORNING, Donovan woke with a backache. After he'd put Nic to bed, he'd gone to talk to Hope, but found the door to their bedroom locked and a pillow and blanket piled in front of it. The couch had been his only option. In the light of the dawning day, he replayed the events of the previous night in his head, hoping that it wasn't as bad as he thought. But that wasn't the case. If the kids had all seen and interacted with Thirteen, it didn't bode well for any of them.

The clock in the kitchen read half past six. If he left now, he could make it to the Dews when they opened at seven. Maybe Lisa had something that would shed some light on the situation and give him a reason to breathe easier. It was bad enough the clock was ticking along at the steady pace, marching him toward Thirteen's forty-eight hour deadline. He needed something, anything, to fix this. Every fiber of his being told him to run, but at his core he knew there wasn't anywhere he could hide that the devil couldn't find. If last night had taught him anything, it was that when Thirteen wanted to find them, he could.

He started the coffee maker for Hope and scribbled a note on the pad she kept by the phone for messages. For the first time in years, he skipped the hassle that was the salt border and blood angel marking. It wasn't worth the time it took now that he knew it didn't do anything to keep Thirteen from walking right up to the front door. Instead, he sped down the mountain roads until he hit the town line and crossed into Belvidere. The roads were dotted with a mixture of old colonial Victorians and newer homes the closer he got to Main Street.

A spot was open right in front of The Daily Dews like it had been waiting for him to arrive, but the chimes on the door were eerily quiet when he entered the store.

"Donovan. I didn't expect to see you so soon." Stan raised a steaming mug in his direction. "What can I get you this morning?"

"Actually, I was hoping that Lisa was around. I had a run in with 'you-know-who' and it turns out the salt didn't work." He scratched the scruff on his chin, made his way toward the register, and chanced a look around to be sure no one was near enough to overhear him. "He gave me an ultimatum."

"You don't say." Stan sipped his coffee and raised his brow.

Donovan rubbed his temples and contemplated the merits of punching the old man in the mouth. "Maybe he's not serious. I mean why would he have to resort to ultimatums? If he wanted to take Daphne he could, right?" The chimes on the door sounded and an older man walked toward the newspaper rack. Donovan dropped his voice as he spoke. "Do you think it's a rouse?"

"Not where the devil is concerned. But you're the fool here looking for a way to beat the devil at a game he's been playing for years."

Donovan's hands fisted at his side. There was no way Stan was going to offer him anything helpful. He needed Lisa. Surely she could offer him something insightful. "I'm not looking to beat him. I just want to protect my family."

"Seems to me that it's a little late to be trying to protect them now. Wasn't the time to protect them before you got in bed with the devil?"

Donovan slammed a fist on the counter, rattling the glass display case below. If he had come in here with any patience, it was now long gone.

"What's going on out here?" Lisa strode through a curtained doorway. Her hand was wrapped in a dishtowel lodged deep within the confines of a glass vase as if she had been midway through doing the dishes. A concerned look creased her face.

"Donny boy came here looking for a way to get out of his deal with the devil. Maybe you can talk some sense into him." With a grunt, Stan walked through the doorway his wife had just come from, but not before dropping a quick kiss on the top of her head.

Lisa finished drying the vase and set it on the

counter. "Don't mind Stan. He's got some hang-ups where," she paused and gave a weary once over to the lone customer in the store before she continued at a whisper, "… 'you-know-who' is concerned." She shooed Donovan away from the register and rung up the man who'd been pouring over the news rack. She waited until the man left the store before speaking again. "So tell me what happened."

Donovan launched into the events of the previous night, leaving nothing out. There was something cathartic about being able to share this burden with someone who truly understood his plight. "So, what do you think it all means?"

She leaned across the counter, her face as close to his ear as she could manage without climbing onto the counter itself. "I think he's looking for the doorway."

Donovan leaned away from the woman and studied her face for any signs of deception. "What doorway? And what does my family have to do with it?"

She shrugged, came out from behind the register, and headed into the back of the store where bookcase after bookcase sat overflowing with leather-bound tomes that looked like they had already withstood the test of time. She waved a hand in his direction and he joined her at a small cafe table nestled amongst the hodge-podge of shelves. A thick, red, leather-bound book sat on the table between them. On the cover was an embossed snake devouring it's own tail encircling a pentagram.

"What's this?"

"My family's book of secrets." Lisa leaned in closer. "This is where I first read the legend of the Devil." She flipped through the time worn pages until the scrawling script became a blur in front of his eyes. "Ah, here it is." She stopped on a page that looked like all the rest except for the crude drawing of a figure with wings, tail, and a forked tongue holding a woman in his arms, tongue flicking over her neck. But the closer Donovan looked at the image it became clear this wasn't the image of a devil about to devour a woman and condemn her to the fires of hell. No, this was the visage of a demon in love—if such a thing was possible. The embrace was tender, possessive, forbidden.

"Who is that?" He pointed to the image.

"That is the woman who started all this: Delila Dewsberry." Confusion contorted her face. "I thought you knew. My family are direct descendants from the woman who gave birth to Drammelech."

A punch to the gut would've been less surprising than the words that had just touched his ears. "Wait. Who's Drammelech?"

"Don't you dare speak his name once you leave this place," Lisa warned. "This place has been spelled and will keep him from entering. But outside of these walls..." She moved her hands to her lap and bowed her head. "I can't promise that saying his name won't be the end of you." She averted her eyes but closed the book with great care.

"I thought you were a Wiccan? How can it be that you are related to the mother of the monster that has been terrorizing my family for decades?"

"It wasn't my choice, I assure you that. Just like I know it wasn't your choice to be a direct line of his." She finally raised her eyes to meet his, the look sharp and wise beyond her years. "Now tell me what he wants from you besides your soul."

It was his turn to cast his eyes down. "It's not just my soul. I also promised him Daphne."

"You what?" Boney fingers clutched his arm to the point of pain. "Tell me you didn't."

"It was a long time ago. And it was to save Hope. He asked for my first born daughter and I agreed."

"What would compel you to do something so stupid?" She released his arm, stood, and began pacing.

"My family has never had anything other than male heirs. I thought it would be a non-issue."

"I see." She stopped pacing and grabbed another book off a nearby shelf. The small book fit easily in her hands and was closed with a ribbon tied around its center. A gentle tug on the loose end of ribbon sent pages fluttering open as if by magic. When the pages stopped their dance, Lisa ran her finger down the opened page without a word. Finally, after more silence than Donovan could stand, she uttered the words he feared most. "Give her to him. It's the only way to make this end."

"No!" His chair toppled over with the force of his refusal. He towered over the woman he had come to like and bared his teeth at her. "There is no way I will give him my daughter. She is innocent in all this." His fingernails dug into the sensitive skin at the palms of his hands.

"If you refuse, then there is nothing to stop him from taking everything from you. He can remove whatever he gave you at the point of contract and then he can take everything that you hold dear. *Everything.*" Lisa set the book down on the table and slid it toward his fisted hands. "This is one of Delila's journals. My family has kept them safe in the event that he ever came for one of us."

"So you know how to stop him?" Hope surged in his chest.

"I know how to stop him from claiming one of Delila's heirs. I can't stop him from claiming any of his own."

The blood circulating through his body froze. There was no way out.

EIGHT

DONOVAN DROVE UP one side of the mountain and down another in the hope that something would change his current situation. His wife doubted him. His children befriended the ultimate deceiver. If he didn't find a way to combat the evil in his life, he would be forced to turn over his thirteen year old daughter to a monster. A little voice in the back of his mind spoke up reminding him that he had an option. All he needed was a willing soul to save Daphne.

Hours passed in the blink of an eye. When he finally got the nerve to face his family, the sun was beginning to set. The house appeared dark when he entered. As he moved through the foyer, the soft glow of the kitchen light sparked to life. He followed the glowing invitation into the kitchen where Hope sat at the table, head in hands.

"Where are the kids, Donny?" She raised her head and gave him a look that was weighted by weariness.

"I don't know." The silence in the house became louder than sirens. Having three children meant there was never silence like this in the house. "Why would you think I would know?" Everything stopped. His heart, his brain, even the blood in his veins stood still.

She rose from her chair and grabbed the table for support. "Because when I woke up today they were gone. I thought you had taken them. I thought after last night you'd lost faith in me and taken them. I've been worried sick all day." Tears streamed down her face and her legs wobbled beneath her.

He wanted to comfort her, to touch her, to soothe away all the hurt, but he knew he'd never be able to heal her in the ways she needed, no, deserved. He'd taken the most beautiful person in the world and twisted and turned it into this shell of a person. Every day of their life together he had unknowingly needled away all the goodness that he loved about her until she was left hollow, used, and discarded.

And now that she was as empty as he had always felt, did he feel any better? Any more human? Any more acceptable? He was as bad for her as her first husband had been. Only instead of just leaving marks on her skin, he left deep welts and scars on her soul. He was no better than the demon that had given him life.

He watched his wife crumple into a heap on the linoleum floor, sobs strangling the breath from leaving her lungs, her limbs slack with grief.

"You gave them to him didn't you? You gave away my babies." Accusation colored every choked syllable.

He couldn't bear her pain any longer. From the corner of his eye, he saw movement in the shadows by the kitchen window. "Stay here. Something's outside," he ordered. He ducked low to the ground and made his way to the back door. Hope's ragged breath echoed in his ears like a bass drum, his heart added the tip-tip-tip of a high hat and the shuffling footsteps on the back porch resonated like a snare. It was unlike Thirteen's footsteps to make noise. Donovan raised his head above the bottom of the window and found two of his three children sneaking across the porch. He watched them disappear around the corner of the house.

Laying a finger across his lips, he rushed toward the powder room. He threw the door open just in time to catch Nic tumbling through the open window, care of a shove from Dax.

For the first time since he had walked through the door, he breathed a sigh of relief. Sure, the boys were about to pay for their transgressions, but at least they were here and safe. He stepped over Nic and grabbed Dax's shoulder as he attempted to catapult himself through the window in his brother's wake.

"What do the two of you think you're doing?"

Startled, Dax looked up and lost his balance. "Ugh, Dad. Hi. We didn't know you were in here."

"I think the better question is what the heck you two are doing in here?" He helped guide Dax through the window and kept him from crashing to the ground on top of his older brother.

Nic scrambled to his feet and kicked the toe of his boot against the floor. "We went out for a while." Neither boy would meet his gaze.

"Out for what? Your mother has been worried sick." Donovan poked his head through the open window and looked for Daphne. "Where's your sister?"

A chorus of, "I don't knows," met his ear.

"What do you mean, you don't know? Didn't she go with you?"

"No." Nic was the first to recover some of his composure. "Dax and I had some guy stuff to work out. We told Daphne to cover for us."

"Yeah," Dax chimed in.

Nic ran his hand through his hair, shaking snow from his shaggy locks as he avoided Donovan's eyes. Dax pulled his hood off his head and a fresh bruise along his jaw came into full view. "What kind of 'guy stuff' were the two of you working out?" Donovan asked as he tilted Dax's chin to get a better look at the bruise.

"Nic wanted to call Callie and ask her to be his girlfriend. I told him I was going to do it. We agreed to fight for her."

"And how did that work out for you?" Donovan retorted. Knowing they had been fighting should've upset him, but neither boy looked too worse for wear.

"What's going on in here?" Hope stood in the doorway and leveled a disapproving look at the three of them.

Both boys muttered, "nothing," under their breath and scooted past her leaving Donovan to squirm under her scrutiny. He placed the screen back into the window, closed the pane, and locked it.

"What about Daphne?"

"They said she was supposed to stay here and cover for them," Donovan answered.

She blocked the doorway and dug her index finger into his chest. "She. Isn't. Here." Each word was punctuated by another poke. "Do they have any idea where she might be?"

Worry lines creased her soft skin. Skin he wanted to caress again; to feel her warmth and enjoy the softness of it beneath the calloused pads of his fingers. What he wouldn't give to be able to have his life be different. His shoulders slumped and he had to admit defeat. He didn't have a clue where their daughter was, and as much as it wasn't directly his fault that she was missing, Hope would never see it any other way.

"I'll get my keys and we'll go looking for her," he offered.

Snow had started falling since he had come home. He brushed the powder off the windshield and started the engine. He flipped on the headlights and noticed that Daphne's bike was missing from its usual spot beside the garage. Hope opened the rear door and waited for the boys to slide in before she closed it and slid into the passenger seat.

"Her bike is gone. Have you any idea where

she might've gone?"

Hope shook her head in answer. Donovan glanced up into the rearview mirror and prayed one of the boys would offer up a plausible option.

"I'm sorry about last night. I'm sorry about everything," he said low enough that only she could hear. He chanced a look at the face he'd loved for the better part of his life. The face he wanted to spend the rest of forever looking at. The face he wasn't sure he'd get to see once his forty-eight hours were up.

After their exchange earlier, there was no doubt in his mind she would never forgive him if he let anything happen to Daphne. If he didn't find her soon, his chances with Hope diminished with every passing second and he feared that Daphne's life would be over before it had really even begun. The play of shadows intertwined with brief bursts of light from passing cars gave her eyes a hollow appearance and deepened the worry lines she wore around her lips. Her silence said everything he already knew; this was the beginning of the end.

He tried again, keeping his voice low so the boys wouldn't hear. "Last night he came to show me that he can come and take Daphne whenever he chooses. I tried to buy more time. He told me that if I found someone with a pure soul willing to part with it of their own free will, he'd give us an extension on taking Daphne."

"And let me guess, you agreed." Her tone sent chills down his spine. He'd never heard her be so harsh. Ever. "Because it's the easy way, isn't it Donny? And the easy way is how you do things."

"Dad," Dax broke the heavy silence. "She and Callie were talking about finding ways to hang out. Maybe she's there."

Realization washed over him. Why hadn't he thought of that? The kids had finally been hand delivered a friend. If the boys had disappeared to fight over Callie, it only made sense that Daphne would go meet her. He stopped the car in the middle of the road and pulled a u-turn to head back into town. The clock on the dash was an ever-present reminder that his time was running out.

NINE

THIS TIME, THERE wasn't an open spot anywhere near The Daily Dews. He circled the block twice before pulling up beside another car and letting Hope out. He watched her walk into the store and was struck by the slump of her shoulders, the shuffle of her step, the tapping of her fingers to her thumb on both hands. It was a tick of hers he had noticed that very first day in the grocery store so many years ago. It had disappeared after her ex-husband had been removed from the picture, but seeing it again was a slap in the face. He had done this to her. He had caused her this pain and there was nothing short of a miracle that could change a damn thing about it.

He idled the car and waited. The boys whispered in the backseat but he couldn't focus on their words. All he could think of was his girls. Daphne. Hope. Daphne. Hope. Something in the pit of his stomach begged him to hold on tight to them for every second he could because they were slipping through his fingers like water. Before long he'd have nothing left. He shuddered at the thought. Movement on the sidewalk created the diversion he desperately needed. A streak of a pink with blonde hair flowing behind approached.

"Callie!" Dax yelled through the closed window before banging the palm of his hand on the glass for emphasis. The girl turned and skidded her bike to a stop.

A low whistle escaped Nic's lips. The girl hopped from her bike and let it fall to the concrete sidewalk.

"Mr. Barren, come quick. It's Daphne, she's in trouble."

He threw the car into park and leapt from the vehicle. His hands wrapped around the girl's arms and shook her, demanding answers to questions that poured from his mouth. It wasn't until he felt the familiar hands of Hope tugging at his arm that he stopped. Shock warred with fear. He stepped back from Calliope, his hands shaking.

"Callie, tell me what happened." Lisa hugged her granddaughter close. "Where were you?"

"Daphne and I met down by the old bridge. We just wanted to spend time together." Her hands flew animatedly as she talked. "But then Daphne started talking to herself. She insisted someone was there, but I didn't see anyone, so I… I…" Calliope's eyes flew wide open and she slapped her hands over her mouth.

"What? You what," Lisa stuttered. "What'd you do?"

Calliope stood on tiptoes and whispered in her grandmother's ear. Donovan watched the exchange, looking for an inkling of what the girl said flash across the older woman's face, but not a single nerve appeared to twitch until the girl stepped back.

"Go inside. Stay with Pops and don't leave the building until I get back. Do you understand?" When the girl only nodded, Lisa asked again. Finally a soft agreement tumbled from Calliope's lips.

"What did she day?" His words were part growl dipped in a healthy dose of snarl. He needed to know, but Lisa just raised a finger, halting his further questions until the girl was safely behind the closed door of the shop.

"We need to go. Now." Lisa hurried to the car and squeezed into the back seat with the boys.

Donovan had the car back in drive before Hope had even shut the door and buckled her seatbelt. "Where to?"

Lisa directed him from the backseat.

"What did Callie say?" Hope asked.

"Just drive. Before it's too late," Lisa retorted.

Donovan took a turn too fast. The car's tires slipped on the fresh snow coating the road and began to skid. He steered into it and straightened the vehicle. The bridge loomed in the distance with street-lights accenting the green steel girders.

"It's up here on the left." Lisa pointed to a small access road before the bridge. As many times as

Donovan had driven near the bridge he'd never noticed the single lane dirt road.

"What's down here?" he asked.

"An abandoned house from the late 1800's that used to be home to the bridge keeper. The position offered a house as part of the salary. It's small, but the town has kept it up and kids sometimes go down there." She reached her hand between the front seats and pointed. "Slow down. It's coming up on the right." The house sat in the dark. Not a single light could be seen inside. A floodlight blinked on as they got closer.

Donovan shifted into park and was out the door before anyone could say a word. It was colder here, which made sense with its close proximity to the Delaware River. Although, something inside him countered that Thirteen was the reason behind the noted drop in temperature. He heard car doors open behind him. "Stay in the car," he yelled over his shoulder. "I've got to do this myself," he muttered to himself.

He stalked around the side of the house. The backyard looked like it was situated precariously close to the cliff that dropped off to the side of the river.

"Daphne," he called. "Are you here?"

"Daddy?" A whimper, scared and meek, answered him.

"Where are you?" He scanned the darkness, but saw nothing.

A door opened at the back of the house and two

figures emerged from the gloom. His eyes struggled to pinpoint where his daughter stopped and Thirteen started, but it was impossible to tell.

"Let her go. I still have twenty-four hours," he called to the devil.

"Ahhh, I was hoping you'd arrive."

Another floodlight blinked on, blinding Donovan as the two crossed the yard. "You said I had two days. Two."

"And you do, but in the meantime, Daphne and I are getting reacquainted." The smile that slid across his face made Donovan sick to his stomach. "Aren't we, Daphne?" Thirteen's tongue flicked between his lips like a snake's testing the air. "Ah, you brought me a snack."

"What?" The crunch of shoes on snow twisted his stomach further. "I told you to stay in the car," he accused. Hope ignored him and walked right past him as if she was possessed. "Hope. No!" He chased after her, but stopped dead in his tracks when he met her icy stare.

"I'm tired, Donny," she called. "I need this to end." She turned back toward Daphne and continued on. "Drammelech," she yelled, "leave my daughter alone." Hope held up a chain twined around her middle finger that twinkled in the night. "You wanted a pure soul, right?"

"No." The word stuck in Donovan's throat like a rotten piece of meat. "No." He tried again but it was a squeak, a mere blip of a sound. "No." It finally ripped from his throat, as if it had been torn from his cursed soul and released into being; a living, breathing thing of its own devices.

"Hush, Donnnnn-ovan," Thirteen scolded. "Let your woman talk." He released Daphne and cocked his head to the side. "Hope, is it?" A laugh erupted from his chest like he'd made the best joke ever. "What have you come to offer me?"

Donovan watched, horrified, as his wife moved ever closer to the monster that owned him.

"I've come to offer you my soul." Each word was laced with a silent strength. Strength she had developed over years of abuse and neglect. Strength she had been cultivating under the surface. Strength she must have known she would need someday to protect her children. She moved within arm's reach of Thirteen.

"Do you offer this gift freely?" His tongue sliced through the air and just barely tested the taste of her skin before it recoiled back into his mouth.

"Yes."

That one single whispered word would haunt Donovan for the rest of his days.

TEN

THIRTEEN STUDIED HOPE, a dubious look on his angular face. Donovan held his breath and waited, feet frozen to the ground, heart pounding in his chest. This couldn't be happening. He had considered that Hope would leave him because of this. Hell, he'd worried about it since the day she told him she was expecting. But he never considered that she would choose to leave him for the Devil. The fucking Devil.

His blood boiled and a twitch overtook him. He broke through whatever fear had held him back and raced to put himself between Thirteen and his wife. "I won't let you. You'll have to go through me first," he spat, anger seething inside of him.

But Thirteen didn't look affected by his words. Instead, he threw his head back and laughed.

"Oh, Donnnnn-ovan. It's too late. She's already agreed." He reached past Donovan and offered a hand to Hope.

Before he could even fully form a thought, Donovan reared back and threw a punch aimed at Thirteen's smug face; a punch that missed hitting anything but that of cold, empty air.

A cackle of laughter split the air behind him. Donovan swung around and there Thirteen stood in all his devilish glory, an arm around Hope.

"Please. Don't." It was half plea, half prayer, but it couldn't go unsaid. He had to fight for something. Even if it had taken him thirty-eight years to learn his lesson. He could not trade one life for another. He couldn't fix one problem by selling off another. He'd already sold his humanity to finally feel the love he'd always wanted, but had never gotten from his parents.

Of course now he understood that his parents were in bed with a devil from before he was born. They didn't have the souls left to offer love. Their faults had been ingrained in him from an early age, and he'd learned that the only way to get what you wanted was to buy it. And no price was too high because there was always this dark figure off in the distance waiting to give you the capital to make the deal. So long as he didn't mind offering up his soul in payment.

But Hope wasn't asking for anything. She hadn't even asked Thirteen if he would hold up his end of the bargain and give Daphne more time. She was blindly trusting the fucking devil and offering him her soul. All for a chance to save their daughter.

Thirteen bent his head, flicked his tongue over

the pulse-point in Hope's neck, and peered up at Donovan through his lashes. "Mmmm." He stood to his full height and Hope shivered in his arms. "You taste like a newborn babe. The Overworld still has a hold on you. I can taste it." Thirteen inhaled the air around Hope and sighed. "Donnnnn-ovan, I accept this willing soul you've brought to me. You have your extension." With a wave of his hand, a scroll appeared in his grasp.

No. No. No, no, no. This couldn't be happening. Donovan knew what came next. His breath sputtered and a sheen of sweat popped to the surface of his skin. Thirteen handed the parchment to Hope and conjured a dagger in his other hand.

Hope didn't even look at the parchment. Instead, she met Thirteen's eyes. "I don't need to read it. I trust you to keep your word. With that faith, I offer myself to you freely." She opened her hand for the dagger. Unlike the swift strike he had made when Donovan had signed his contract, Thirteen handed over the blade and took the parchment. Donovan had never known him to part with the instrument.

Unable to peel his eyes away, he watched as the love of his life lifted the dagger, weighing it in her hand. Donovan wished she would look at him and not Thirteen, but she never moved her eyes from the devil's. She dragged the edge of the blade across the palm of her left hand until it sliced through her tender skin and beads of blood bubbled to the surface. She never winced and her gaze never faltered. Watching her in this moment was one of the most beautiful memories he would ever have.

Hope turned the dagger and offered it, handle first, to Thirteen. "You're turn, Drammelech." She nodded toward the offered blade.

In the artificial glow of the floodlight, his eyes gleamed. "Ah, you offer me so much pleasssss-ure dear." He bent and sniffed the blood that pooled in her hand. "You first." He opened the parchment and guided her hand in his over the scroll. A gentle tip of her hand was enough to cause her blood to run over her skin and land on the contract. He turned her hand back to its original position, raised it to his lips, and licked the wound.

The play of emotions that rolled over Thirteen's face sickened Donovan but there was nothing more that could be done. He dropped to his knees in the snow, tears pouring down his cheeks. There was no going back now.

Thirteen reached for the offered dagger but Hope spoke before his fingers could grasp it.

"May I say goodbye first?"

Thirteen eyed her, suspicion obvious in his contorted face, but nodded in agreement.

Donovan swiped the tears from his face and tried to pull himself together. He needed to find the words to tell her—to tell her what? Thanks? That he loved her? He squinted against a fresh stream of tears threatening to overflow his eyes. He waited to hear her footsteps near but silence met his ears. He looked up only to see Hope waving Daphne over to her. She hugged her tight. Daphne's shoulders rose and fell in time with the rivulets of tears that fled down her cheeks. Hope pulled from the embrace and placed a kiss on her daughter's cheek. Daphne surged forward and threw her arms around Hope's neck. Through the sheen of his own tears, he watched as Hope's hand slipped into the front pocket of Daphne's jacket. When she withdrew it, the chain that had been dangling in her grasp was gone. Hope placed one last kiss on Daphne's cheek, then stepped back and pointed toward Donovan. Daphne turned in his direction and Hope graced him with a small smile before turning back toward Thirteen.

"Thank you."

He looked pleased. "You will make me very happy, Hope." He curled his palm around the dagger's blade and pulled until a stream of blood followed. Thick wet drops landed on the parchment.

Donovan grabbed Daphne's quaking body and hugged her tight. He pushed her head into his shoulder because she didn't need to witness this. She would need to remember her mother as the brave woman who sacrificed herself to the devil to save her daughter.

Satisfied, Thirteen re-rolled the scroll and licked his tongue across the dagger. "This will give me great pleasssss-ure, I assure you. Unfortunately, I can't say the same for you, dear." Hope bowed her head under the weight of his words. "I've always wanted a freely given soul. I was told it would taste like the nectar of the godssssss." His face lowered and thin lips pursed toward her. A finger tilted her head up to give him the access he needed and then Thirteen laid his lips across hers.

A protest died in Donovan's throat as Hope's knees buckled beneath her. He was torn between going to his wife and shielding his daughter's eyes from watching this.

A guttural and inhuman sound erupted from Thirteen; a sound that ricocheted off every solid surface and reverberated unfettered until it mingled with a whimper in perfect harmony. Donovan squeezed his eyes closed against the scene. He couldn't watch any longer. The Hope he had loved was being ripped from her body. This time the devil wasn't leaving her soul intact but marked like he had with Donovan. No, he was pulling it from her living, breathing, loving body. And he was enjoying every moment of it.

ELEVEN

A SOFT THUD pulled Donovan back to reality. He opened his eyes in time to see Hope wilt lifelessly to the ground. Thirteen was nowhere to be seen.

"Mom." A scream rose from behind him. Startled, he turned to see the boys running full speed toward Hope's body.

"Don't touch her," Donovan warned. He released Daphne and started after them.

Nic and Dax stood over Hope, tears ran down their faces. "How could you? How could you let that monster do that to mom?" Dax whirled around, accusation and hatred clung to his every word. "You let him kill her."

Donovan reached a hand toward his youngest son and was rewarded with a shove that landed him in the snow.

"Don't you dare touch me," Dax seethed. "You ruin everything."

"Dax…"

"Shut up. You have no right to speak to me. You just let him take her. We saw you stand there and do nothing."

Realization dawned deep and painful in his gut. The boys hadn't listened. They had followed their mother from the car and watched every horrid moment. "I'm sorry."

The words were insufficient even to his ears. They weren't enough, but they were all he could offer.

A warm hand rested on his shoulder as he watched the light go out in his son's eyes. "Donovan, there's nothing you can do now." Lisa stood beside him, understanding flowing off her like a cape. "Let's get her back to the car and we can take care of it from there."

He gathered himself and rose from the ground, determination setting into his bones. Lisa was right; he couldn't leave Hope here in this snowy grave. He bent beside her and took a good look at his wife; the first since last night. Dark circles ringed her eyes. Had she not slept the night before? Her lips were pink but would soon turn blue from the lack of oxygen-rich blood pumping through her system. Her eyes stared unfocused at the night sky. He bowed his head and laid a gentle kiss on her lips. He didn't want the last lips to touch hers to be evil. She deserved better than that. A puff of warm breath tickled his face. He sat back on his heels, shock sinking in. He ran a hand across her brow. Still warm. He leaned close again and the steady whiff of her breath skimmed over his skin. He pressed his first two fingers to her neck and searched for the telltale pulse of heart. It bumped against his fingers and hope surged through his system. It couldn't be… She was alive. Alive?

"Lisa, come quick. She's still breathing." His pulse raced, the rest of the world melting away. Hope was alive.

Lisa pushed through the blockade that Donovan's boys made and knelt. "Hope, can you hear me? It's Lisa." She shook Hope's arm again but there was no response. "Donovan," she whispered and leaned across Hope's unresponsive body. "Something isn't right. She's breathing and her heart is beating, but she's empty. I can't feel a trace of essence inside her."

"What?" Confused, he tried to make sense of her words.

"Her essence. Spirit. Soul. Whatever it is that makes her who she is. It's missing. I can feel the emptiness." She smoothed the hair from Hope's face like a mother would do to a sleeping child. "We need to get her some medical attention, but you need to know that this can't last forever. Eventually her body will grow tired and she will slip away."

The words hung heavy in the air. "I see." He nodded, but refused to believe there wasn't more that could be done. Hope had shown faith. Now it was his turn to do the same. He carefully lifted her into his arms and carried his beloved to the car. He tucked her into the passenger seat and snapped her buckle as if it was as normal as breathing.

"Dad?" Daphne laid a hand on his arm.

"Yeah?"

"She asked me to tell you that she knew what she was doing." She twisted her hands together.

He pulled his daughter into his arms and held her tight. He could do this. No, he *would* do this. For Hope. For the kids. For the love that he'd never before realized he'd had all along inside him. He'd do whatever it took to save her.

TWELVE

THREE WEEKS LATER...

DONOVAN FOUND HIMSELF at The Dews in the same seat he had been the day before. A large tome sat on the table in front of him. His eyes were tired, weary, and playing tricks on him as he reread the passage before him and hoped this time he would remember it.

"Lisa, I think I found something here," he called. For the last few weeks he'd parked himself in this very spot and combed through book after book of occult topics looking for a way to find Thirteen. He'd called for him directly. He'd even dared to speak his forbidden name. But nothing. Not a word. Not a cold breeze. Nothing. So, here he came every day to read. Lisa no longer sat with him while he poured over yet another book. Instead, she went about her day minding the store. Stan had finally stopped glaring at him and would now bring him a cup of black coffee once he cracked his first book of the day.

"Donovan, it's almost time to get the kids from school." Lisa closed the book he was reading. "Why don't you leave this for tomorrow? It will still be here then. Besides, have you done your holiday shopping yet? You do remember that Christmas is in a few weeks?"

He ran a hand through his hair. Hope used to take care of the holiday things. She also made dinners, taught school, and made sure there was clean underwear. Thankfully, Daphne had stepped up to help with the cooking. He never realized how much she enjoyed it before now. Nic had even taken over laundry duty. There were a few pink garments that came about the first time or two, but he seemed to have a rhythm with it now. Dax, on the other hand, appeared content to hold the longest grudge of his life.

He hadn't spoken a word outside of what was demanded of him since the night that Hope… Well, left. He still couldn't bring himself to say that she died, because it wasn't true. She was alive. She was hooked up to monitors and machines to keep her that way. Doctors claimed it was a catatonic state. They felt very confident that she could come out of it any day now.

What the doctors didn't know was that the Devil had her soul, her essence, her very life force. Without that being returned to her she would remain this way forever; the machines beeping and marking the days until her body wore out.

"Thanks for the reminder, Lisa. I'll do the shopping this weekend with the kids." He reopened the book and thumbed back to the beginning of the section about soul-eaters. It was the most promising passage he'd encountered yet, describing an act very similar to what Thirteen had done to Hope. The passage stated that a soul freely given could be returned. There was a ritual involving the ceremonial knife from the soul-eating process that was documented to have a favorable outcome where the person who received their soul didn't lose their mind afterward. Promising wasn't the same as positive, but at this point he'd take promising over nothing.

He slid a sheet of paper in the book to mark his spot and stood. "See you tomorrow, Lisa." He nodded to Stan on his way out the door.

One more night. If he could just get through one more night then maybe he could make headway tomorrow. He repeated the mantra over and over again in his head as he drove home to meet the kids off the bus. All he needed was a sign that everything would be okay.

A few minutes later the kids were bustling about doing homework, chores, and picking at one another. In a previous time he could almost believe things were normal. The phone rang in the kitchen and three sets of feet went running for it. That was one thing he hadn't yet adjusted to. Their social lives had blossomed in the short while since starting at public school. Most weekends there were sleepovers and outings to the movie theater—normal things that normal kids did. Only now his kids were even less normal than before. Not only were they direct descendants of Thirteen, but their mother was essentially being held captive by him. One day he would come for each of them. Of that, Donovan was certain. He just had to teach them how to be resilient against Thirteen's charms.

That evening, Donovan stood in the doorway to the twins' bedroom and said his usual goodnight. He made his way down the hall to Daphne's room and went through the same motions all over again.

But before he could leave, she called him closer.

"Daddy?"

She rarely called him that these days unless she was under stress. "What, princess?" He sat on the edge of her bed.

"You need to stop looking for him." Her voice was low and shook when she spoke.

"What?" Donovan couldn't be positive that he heard her. He studied his daughter in the darkened room and noticed she was shivering.

"Stop looking for him," she repeated. "The devil," she whispered for clarification. "You need to stop. *He* knows you're looking for him and he's playing with you. He wants you to find him so he can have me. As long as you stop looking them he can't have me. At least not for a while."

"Where did you hear that?" Donovan asked. "Did he tell you this?" As much as it pained him to think that Thirteen was stalking his daughter still, he needed to know if he was the source of her information.

"No, Daddy." She shook her head. "Remember that night?" she hedged.

"Yes. Of course."

"Well, a few days ago I found something in my pocket. At first I didn't recognize it, but then I remembered mom holding it when she…when she…" Emotion bubbled over and her words got caught in her throat. Instead of trying for words, she pulled a pendant from around her neck.

Donovan switched on the bedside lamp and lifted the pendant closer. It looked familiar. A scaled serpent formed a circle by eating its tail. At the center of the circle was a pale grey stone, cool to the touch with a small pentagram carved at the middle. He knew he'd seen it before but he couldn't place where.

"I don't remember your mom having this before that night."

"I don't either. But Dad, when Callie saw it, she said it would keep…" She looked from side to side then leaned in, "keep *him* from seeing me. But I've seen him. Not here, but in my dreams I see him. And mom. And she told me to tell you to stop looking for him. That has to mean something, right?"

Bile crept up Donovan's throat and he struggled to push it back. He released the pendant and watched it fall to his daughter's skin. "I don't know what it means, but tomorrow I'll ask around and find out. In the meantime, do as your mother says and keep it on at all times. Okay?"

"Okay, Dad."

"I'm serious, kiddo. Under no circumstances can you take it off. Understood?"

"Yeah, I got it." She gave him a peck on the cheek and then snuggled beneath her covers. "See you in the morning."

"Goodnight, princess." He turned off the lamp and shut the door behind him.

The next morning Donovan dropped the kids off at school on his way to The Dews. He had to talk to Lisa and see if she could shed any light on the pendant. Within moments, she had pulled out a book that looked familiar; a book of secrets he remembered her talking about once before. She flipped through the first pages until she found what she was looking for, then turned the book and showed him a drawing of the pendant.

"I gave it to Hope that night," Lisa explained. "I thought it would keep her safe. It was supposed to allow her to see him even though he didn't own her soul and protect her from him." She bowed her head. "I guess it didn't work as advertised."

"Hope gave it to Daphne before he took her soul. And now that Daphne's wearing it, she can see Thirteen and Hope when she dreams. She said Hope's been talking to her."

"Well, based on all the books I've read on the subject, Drammelech's mother saw him talking to what looked like nothing after his father was cursed to the Underworld, so maybe there is something to Daphne's dreams. Unlike his father, Drammelech is stuck in this realm and unable to walk between the worlds. Delila created this symbol to be able to keep an eye on him but also to hide herself in plain sight from him. Being that he is part witch and part demon, he can't enter into the Underworld or the Overworld without using a portal. And every portal has a key."

Lisa flipped further through the book until she found what she was looking for. She turned it so that Donovan could read the passage for himself. The handwriting was small and faded, but he could make out the words of a prophecy written long ago.

To unlock the gate between heaven and hell, a female descendant must walk between the worlds and bring with her a symbol of each. With those tokens she will be able to offer admittance to any being on any side of the veils so long as she remains pure of heart.

"Daphne. That's what he wants her for. He wants her to unlock the portal into Hell." Dread hit him in the chest, stealing his breath away.

"Or worse," Lisa added. "Imagine if the son of the Devil, who is a devil in his own right, was allowed access to heaven. The Overworld would be vulnerable to potential attack. I'm not sure what you believe, but I was raised to believe there is a fine line separating the light from the darkness. If darkness is allowed into the light, both will fade away into nothingness. We can't let that happen, Donovan." She paused and studied him, fire burning in her eyes. "Not even to save Hope."

THIRTEEN

FIVE YEARS LATER...

SUMMER WAS JUST around the corner. Donovan felt it in his very core and it inspired hope. Hope that this year would be different. Hope that he would finally be able to track down Thirteen and reclaim the soul that his wife so desperately needed. Hope that his family could go back to the way it had been before Hope had sacrificed herself.

Noise from upstairs pulled him from his thoughts. A squeal followed by running footsteps was a welcome distraction. Especially now that he knew the house would soon be pregnant with silence. A door slammed while Daphne yelled and Nic laughed. It was a symphony of sounds that mimicked normalcy. Donovan scooped ground coffee into the coffeepot and turned it on. It would be a good day. The kids were safe, they were grown, and today they would each cross the threshold into adulthood with the movement of a tassel on a cap.

Heavy footsteps thundered down the stairs. The herd of elephant sounds would be missed when the triplets each went off to their new destinations. Dax shouldered his way past Donovan on his path to the fridge. The kitchen wasn't small, but Dax seemed intent on making one last attempt to ensure that Donovan knew how angry his middle child was. For the last five years Dax had gone to great lengths to throw every bad thing in his adolescent life in Donovan's face like it was a direct result of Hope's catatonic state. The state she would never come out of until he found a way to return her soul to her body. The very same state her body fought to maintain, almost like she knew she had something to hold on for.

If he had known that her selfless sacrifice would end with him having the equivalent of a zombie for a wife, he might've done something different. He never considered something this barbaric would happen when she offered up her soul in exchange for thirteen more years of safety for their daughter? He hadn't gone catatonic when he'd signed over his soul, but years of research turned up only the vaguest of answers as to why. Hope's soul had been pure, unlike his when he'd made his deal. Therefore, hers was more valuable to the likes of Thirteen and his Devil-of-a-dad. With a pure soul like hers, they couldn't risk taking it and leaving her any of her humanity left intact, because if the legends were to be believed and she were allowed to go on living a soulless but still human existence, her good deeds and pure heart could revoke the deal and leave them empty handed.

His pure-hearted daughter was the prize Thirteen was after—some magical key that was more valuable than all the riches in the world. Of course it made sense that Thirteen would trade one for the other at some point, but until Donovan had a way to rid the world of Thirteen he couldn't take the chance with Hope's soul and let him get his hands on Daphne either.

Thirteen wouldn't leave himself open to that option. Not with Daphne still free from his grasp. Donovan spent many late nights pouring over ancient texts at The Dews. He'd looked for a way to save Hope's soul of course, but he'd also looked for a way to break the curse that had gotten him into this in the first place.

All he had to show for his dedication was bags under his eyes and the knowledge that the Devil took deals seriously. The Devil kept his end as long as the humans involved in the deal kept theirs. So to honor his beloved wife, Donovan stopped trying spells to reclaim her soul. He stopped dangerous treks into the Pine Barrens in search of Thirteen's lair. He stopped looking over Daphne's shoulder. She would remain safe as long as Hope's soul was in Thirteen's possession and Daphne wore the pendant forged by Thirteen's own mother. Besides, Donovan had no intention of making Hope's sacrifice meaningless.

As if she knew he was thinking about her, Daphne burst into the kitchen, her hair flying in every direction with her oldest brother hot on her heels.

"I'm driving." Laughter tangled with dance steps that looked out of place in the kitchen.

"Like hell you are," Nic protested. "You cheated."

"Did not," she countered, a spin of her body had her headed toward the back door.

"I told Opie I'd pick her up," Nic groaned. "If you drive, she'll sit up front with you."

"Not my fault the girl has a weak stomach and can't ride in the back," his daughter retorted.

Donovan watched Nic make a grab for the keys and miss. He shook his head. Even at eighteen the triplets reminded him of their younger selves. From the corner of his eye he saw Dax take a swig straight from the orange juice container. He knew good and well that it was unacceptable but Donovan ignored it just like Dax's other passive aggressive slights over the last months. There was only so much he could do now that they were grown. Besides, he was grateful that Dax hadn't run off the day of his birthday. Instead, he stayed around and finished the school year with a sour disposition and an increasing level of defiance.

The kitchen phone rang, calling a halt to the antics of all three. Donovan watched them turn competitive looks toward one another. The mad dash was one he loved to hate. Ever since he enrolled them in the public schools and they made friends, the phone was a weapon they used against one another. Looking back, he didn't know what he and Hope had been thinking keeping the children so isolated. The children blossomed into lovely people with the influence of others and nothing changed about their innate good hearts. But when that phone rang they all pounced on the counter with the grace of baby elephants. And over the years, they all hoped to hear the same voice on the other end of the line: Calliope's.

Dax got to it first and snatched the handset from the cradle. "Yo." The greeting was surly, but when his lips pulled wide Donovan knew it was

Callie. She was the only thing that made his youngest son smile these days. "Sure I'll come get you. Is the bike okay? Daphne has the car." The white lie slipped through his lips without even a trace of guilt on his face and Donovan cringed. Dax put the handset back in the cradle with a triumphant *thunk* then stuck his tongue out at his siblings. "Sorry, losers. Looks like Callie was looking for a change of pace today," Dax bragged.

Maybe some darkness had crept into his children after all. Nic's shoulders deflated and Daphne bit her lip to keep quiet while Dax grabbed an extra leather jacket from a hook by the door and threw it over his shoulder. He had worked a lot of overtime at a local gas station and auto shop to afford the late model Harley he prided himself in restoring it to its original glory. Some extra overtime allowed him to buy a nice leather jacket that he always took when he knew he'd be driving Callie anywhere. Maybe Hope had been right the first night about those two.

Dax sauntered from the house without a word and Nic grumbled under his breath. Daphne patted his shoulder and whispered something in his ear that brought a smile to his face. Donovan just watched, pleased that they had one another. Pleased that they were growing into fine young adults. Pleased that they would someday be able to stand on their own two feet without him. Because he could feel in his gut that the day was coming that he would finally go head to head with Thirteen. The likelihood of a victory was miniscule.

Hours later, Donovan stood in the setting sun and watched his children whooping and hollering with their friends as caps flew in the air around them. His heart grew heavy watching them. Hope would've loved this. She would've wanted to capture every moment on film so that it could be forever locked away in her memory. Donovan stuffed his hands into his pockets and just watched. Being the loner he was, Donovan witnessed something that he knew would forever change the lives of his kids.

Off to the side of the crowd surrounding the new graduates stood a man dressed in a dark suit. Beside him stood the ethereal image of a woman that Donovan would recognize anywhere. The man raised a single hand in salute then slid it around the shoulders of the woman by his side. Bile rose in Donovan's throat, burning and acidic. He watched as Thirteen caressed Hope's arms and kissed at her neck. It couldn't be. Donovan knew his wife was safe and sound at the facility the next town over under the watchful eyes of medical personnel.

This must be some illusion Thirteen created to torture him with. Then a hoot came from the center of the football field-turned-graduation stadium. In the center of the mass of kids were Dax and Callie. His hands were tangled in her long mane of curls and his lips were pressed to hers in a passionate display.

Donovan blinked and turned his attention back to where Thirteen had been, but he was gone. In his place was an empty void in the crowd. There was no denying that Donovan's life was anything other than extraordinary. But it wasn't extraordinary in the way he would've wished and dreamed for. Instead, here he stood, heart lodged in his throat, wishing he never laid eyes on Hope. As his father once told him, having hope would be his undoing. Now he knew truer words had never been spoken.

BIOGRAPHY

JENI BURNS is a Jersey girl living in a southern world. While she's firmly planted in the South with her husband, two kids, and one massive poodle, her heart lives in the Northwestern part of New Jersey where her characters reside. Since writing about home is cheaper than airfare, she spends much of her time living vicariously in NJ's snowy winters and humidity-free summers.

Jeni has been telling stories since she first learned to string two words together. Thanks to her mom and her middle school English teacher both telling her she should be a writer, she now happily spends her days writing all the stories that continuously float around in her head while drinking fabulous decaf coffees.

DID YOU GET *Betrayed* by Dema? If not, read the first chapter of *Sacrificed*'s prequel now.

BETRAYED

ONE

EARLY 1700's

DELILA DEWSBERRY LIVED a simple life. It didn't mean that it was an unhappy life, but it wasn't a particularly fulfilling one either. As was the custom of the time, Delila had been married before she could slip too far into her teens and be too old for the task, which left her with years of experience in darning, butter churning, and child rearing. Although, these skills didn't give her the satisfaction she had dreamed her life would provide.

Her husband, Thomas, was a reputable man with a well-producing farm and a rotund midsection. Her parents had made the deal with little consideration for her opinion on the matter, but here she was living the life she'd been dealt by Fate, or God, or God-forbid the Goddess.

Delila didn't dare think the word Goddess too

often, and she never uttered it aloud. In superstitious times like these, the mere mention of a being other than God would get you stoned, or worse, burned at the stake; and knowing her husband the way she did, Delila knew he would be the first to light the pylon. So Delila kept her beliefs, and her gifts, to herself. Not even Thomas, who slept beside her every night, would guess there was more to her simple life. On solstice nights, she snuck from her bed to perform the spells that kept the land fertile and the livestock well fed. Without her gifts, the farm would have turned into a worthless plot of land long ago.

Soon it would be time to celebrate the date of their betrothal. If Delila had her way, she'd be with child again soon. It did not matter how often she begged for Thomas to take advantage of his marital rites in the last three years, he always balked at the idea. Which is why she had taken to be-spelling him on their anniversary so that she could have one night of passion. Besides, if there was ever a time her husband should want her, she believed the anniversary of their betrothal was it. The need was worth the risk of being discovered a witch.

Their one night of passion was worth the risk of the stockade to combat Delila's loneliness that spanned the other three hundred sixty four nights of the year. It hadn't always taken such lengths to get her husband to notice her, but after stumbling upon Thomas and a farm hand in a passionate embrace, it had become routine for him to turn her away night after night. The allure his lover offered to Thomas had become a constant and growing source of discontent in Delila's life. On more nights that not, she yearned for something more; something greater than her current predicament could offer. Fortunately for her, and Thomas as well she supposed, she developed a new tincture that she believed would finally not only make him amorous, but also produce a child. If all went according to her plan, not only would a child breathe new life into her marriage, but also send Thomas's lover back to wherever he had come from with the outward proof of Thomas and Delila's coupling.

Delila added an extra pinch of powdered oyster to the tincture she ground together and smiled. She had often asked Thomas to convert the extra room out in the barn into a place where she could play with the tools of her father's trade, shaping ordinary things into wearable art, but he always scoffed. To Thomas, a woman's place was in the home caring for her children, not out in some barn whittling hours away on something that men did. So, while he worked, she stole away to the barn and did as she pleased in a makeshift workshop, hopeful that he would never learn of her deception.

With the exception of his infidelity, Thomas was very devout in his beliefs. Beliefs that raised their sons to be God-fearing men and their daughters to be man-serving wives.

Fifteen years into their sham of a marriage, Delila was tired of being a mother to babies, but babies were the only reason Thomas would take her to his side of their marital bed and make her feel whole. The kind of whole she dreamed of being; feminine, purposeful, powerful. To have that she would do what society dictated as conventional. She'd have children and look after a man who loved another; until the man of her dreams came for her, and come for her he would. At least, she hoped he would. This late in her life she often wondered if the mystery man who had wandered through her dreams since childhood, beckoning her to join him, was nothing more than a dream. A dream that promised love, laughter, and excitement. It was those visions that drove her forward, closer to him.

Her destiny.

Her escape.

In the meantime, Delila handed off the day to day routines of childrearing and housework to her eldest daughter, Esther, who was soon of age to be a bride herself. Delila instead, took the time to journal new spells and tinctures including her newest fertility potion. She also found reasons to sneak into the woods surrounding the pastures to spy on Thomas. Something about catching her adulterous husband with the look of love in his eye drove her. To what she still didn't know, but she found herself spending much time comparing herself to the man Thomas so often embraced while she tinkered in her workshop. He, like Thomas, was broad, and when it came to disposition he was abrasive and powerful, even though his station in life made Thomas his superior. Studying them during those intimate times only drove her to desperation; desperation for a lover of her own, one who understood her needs and could fulfill her, making her life all the things it currently was not.

Although it was often said in the company of the womenfolk of the church that keeping secrets from one's spouse opened a door to the devil, Delila didn't believe in such hogwash. It was well known in her family that the devil was just the balancing point for the Goddess.

Without light, dark cannot exist, and the opposite was surely true. Light always shined brightest in a dark room. In the days leading up to her anniversary, Delila often found times to excuse herself from the house, disappearing into the barn. It was there in the solitude she reworked her tincture, a love potion of sorts, and found pleasure at her own hand.

Up until recently, Thomas rarely spoke of the children's existence at all, despite there being twelve of them. Thomas had recently taken to showing their eldest son, Thomas Jr, the ropes around the farm. She would often watch Thomas grooming him to one day take over the responsibility that lay solely on his thick shoulders. But there was never any warmth in it. By day's end both would return to the house weary-eyed and silent. It often made her wonder what it was that Thomas was teaching him.

One day while tinkering in the barn, Delila looked up to find a man standing in the doorway watching her. The appearance of a strange man should've startled her, but her heart raced as excitement coursed through her body. She had known he would come.

Not for a second did she doubt that this was the man from her lifelong visions. Visions that she thought were premonitions of her future husband. Visions she thought had wronged her upon meeting Thomas. Visions that still plagued her on warm summer nights when her lust carried her off into dreams too heated to confess. She could never share these visions with anyone for fear that she'd find herself strung up in an orchard one day, but it didn't keep her from making note when she had them in her journals, and this man was one of her more favored delights.

Unlike Thomas, he was young and hard in the middle, made of muscle and sinew. He stood taller than any man she had ever laid eyes on, and exuded a sense of power. A power she desperately wanted in her life. A power that made her weak in the knees. A power she could claim as her own and not be struck down for possessing.

In her visions he never spoke, yet something about him gave Delila reason to believe his voice would be low, dark, and thick like molasses. The sun behind him played shadows over his face in the peaks and valleys of his sharp features, and even though they had never before spoken, Delila knew him. She knew him body and soul, and she knew his patience would wan quickly if she didn't go to him immediately.

And go to him she did.

Available for purchase on Amazon.

Want a sneak peek at what's coming next for Elech?

Visit www.jeniburns.com

For an exclusive excerpt of *Revealed*, the third
Twisted Fate Novella

www.ingramcontent.com/pod-product-compliance
Lightning Source LLC
Chambersburg PA
CBHW020420130626
46549CB00006B/2667